WAIT TILL HELEN COMES

A GHOST STORY

MARY DOWNING HAHN

AN AVON CAMELOT BOOK

AVON BOOKS, INC.
1350 Avenue of the Americas
New York, New York 10019

A Ghost Story for Norm

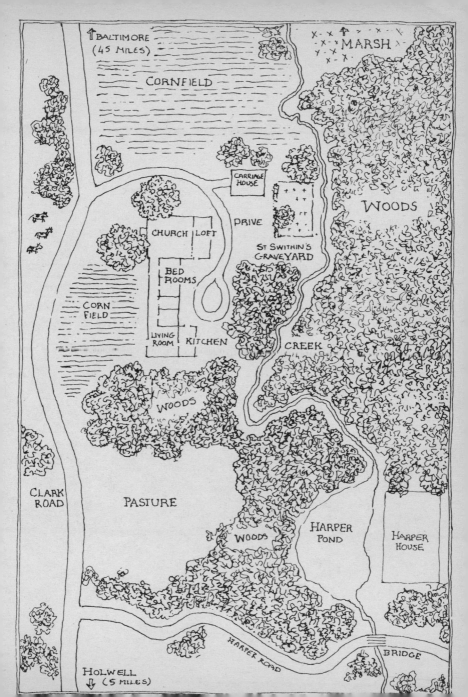

1

"YOU'VE BOUGHT a church?" Michael and I looked up from the pile of homework covering most of the kitchen table. I was in the middle of writing a poem for Mr. Pelowski's English class, and Michael was working his way happily through twenty math questions.

Mom filled a kettle with water and put it on the stove. Her cheeks were pink from the March wind, and so was the tip of her nose. "You and Molly will love it," she promised. "It's exactly the sort of place Dave and I have been looking for all winter. There's a carriage house for him to use as a pottery workshop and space in the choir loft for me to set up a studio. It's perfect."

"But how can we live in a church?" Michael persisted, refusing to be won over by her enthusiasm.

"Oh, it's not really a church anymore," Mom said. "Some people from Philadelphia bought it last year and built an addition on the side for living quarters. They were going to set up an antique store in the actual church, but, after doing all that work, they decided they didn't like living in the country after all."

"It's out in the country?" I frowned at the little cat I was doodling in the margin of my notebook paper.

Mom smiled and gazed past me, out our kitchen window and into Mrs. Overton's window directly across the alley. I had a feeling she was seeing herself standing in front of an easel, working on one of her huge oil paintings, far from what she called the "soul-killing life of the city." She has a maddening habit of drifting away into her private dream world just when you need her most.

"Where *is* the church?" I asked loudly.

"Where is it?" Mom poured boiling water into her cup and added honey. "It's in Holwell, Maryland, not far from the mountains. It's beautiful. Just beautiful. The perfect place for painting and potting."

"But what about Molly and me? What are we supposed to do while you and Dave paint and make pottery?" Michael asked.

"You promised I could be in the enrichment program this summer," I said, thinking about the creative writing class I was planning to take. "Will I still be able to?"

"Yes, and what about Science Club?" Michael asked. "I'm already signed up for it. Mr. Phillips is going to take us to the Aquarium and the Science Center and even to the Smithsonian in Washington."

Mom sighed and shook her head. "I'm afraid you two will have to make other plans for summer. We'll be moving in June, and I can't possibly drive all the way back to Baltimore every day."

"But I've been looking forward to Science Club all year!" Michael's voice rose, and I could tell he was trying hard not to cry.

"You'll have plenty of woods to explore," Mom said calmly. "Just think of all the wildlife you can observe and the insects you can add to your collection. Why, the day Dave and I were there, we saw a raccoon, a possum, a woodchuck, and dozens of squirrels." Mom leaned across the table, smiling, hoping to convince Michael that he was going to love living in a church way out in the country, miles away from Mr. Phillips and Science Club.

But Michael wasn't easy to convince. Slumping down in his chair, he mumbled, "I'd rather stay in Baltimore, even if I never see anything but cockroaches, pigeons, and rats."

"Oh, for heaven's sake, Michael!" Mom looked exasperated. "You're ten years old. Act like it!"

As Michael opened his mouth to defend himself, Heather appeared in the kitchen doorway, responding, no doubt, to her built-in radar for detecting trouble. Her pale gray eyes roved from Mom to Michael, then to me, and back again to Mom. From the expression on her face, I imagined she was hoping to witness bloodshed, screams, a ghastly scene of domestic violence.

"Why, Heather, I was wondering where you were!" Mom turned to her, infusing her voice with enthusiasm again. "Guess what? Your daddy and I have found a new place for us to live, way out in the country. Won't that be fun?" She gave Heather a dazzling Romper-Room smile and reached out to embrace her.

With the skill of a cat, Heather sidestepped Mom's arms and peered out the kitchen window. "Daddy's home," she announced without looking at us.

"Oh, no, I forgot to put the casserole in the oven!" Mom ran to the refrigerator and pulled out a concoction of eggplant, cheese, tomatoes, and bulgur and shoved it into the oven just as

Dave opened the back door, bringing a blast of cold March air into the room with him.

After giving Mom a hug and a kiss, he swooped Heather up into his arms. "How's my girl?" he boomed.

Heather twined her arms possessively around his neck and smiled coyly. "They were fighting," she said, darting a look at Michael and me.

Dave glanced at Mom, and she smiled and shook her head. "We were just discussing our big move to the country, that's all. Nobody was *fighting*, Heather." Mom turned on the cold water and began rinsing lettuce leaves for a salad.

"I don't like it when they fight." Heather tightened her grip on Dave's neck.

"Come on, Michael." I stood up and started gathering my books and papers together. "Let's finish our homework downstairs."

"Dinner will be ready in about half an hour," Mom called after us as we started down the basement steps.

As soon as we were safely out of everybody's hearing range, I turned to Michael. "What are we going to do?"

He flopped down on the old couch in front of the television. "Nothing. It's too late, Molly. They've bought the church and we're moving there. Period."

Grabbing a pillow, he tossed it across the room, narrowly missing one of Mom's paintings, a huge close-up of a sunflower. "Why did she have to marry him? We were perfectly happy before he and Heather came along."

I slumped beside him, nodding my head in agreement. "They've ruined everything." Glancing at the stairs to make sure Heather hadn't sneaked down to spy on us, I said, "If only Heather was a normal kid. She acts more like a two-year-old than a seven-year-old. And she's mean; she tattles and lies and does everything she can to get us in trouble with Dave. Why do they always take her side — even Mom?"

Michael made a face. "You know what Dave says." Making his voice deep and serious, he said, "Heather is an unusually imaginative and sensitive child. And she has suffered a great loss. You and Molly must be patient with her."

I groaned. "How long can we feel sorry for her and be nice to her? I know it must have been horrible to see her mother die in a fire and be too little to help, but she was only three years old. She should've gotten over it by now, Michael."

He nodded. "If Dave would take her to a shrink, I bet she would get better. My friend Martin's little brother goes to some guy out in Towson, and it's helped him a lot. He plays with dolls and draws pictures and makes things out of clay."

I sighed. "You know perfectly well what Dave thinks of shrinks, Michael. I heard him tell Mom that all they do is mess up your head."

Michael got up and flipped the TV to "Speed Racer." With one eye on the screen, he set about doing the rest of his math while I sat there doodling more cats instead of finishing my poem.

After a few minutes, I nudged Michael. "Do you remember that movie we saw on TV about the little girl who did horrible things to her enemies?"

"*The Bad Seed?*"

"Yes, that was it. Well, sometimes I think Heather's like that girl, Rhoda. Suppose she burned her mother up on purpose the way Rhoda burned up the janitor?"

Michael peered at me over the top of his glasses. "You're crazy, Molly. No three-year-old kid could do anything like that." He was speaking to me as if he were a scientist explaining something to a child instead of a ten-year-old boy addressing his twelve-year-old sister.

Realizing how ridiculous I sounded, I laughed and said, "Just kidding," but I really wasn't. There was something about Heather that made me truly uncomfortable. No matter how hard I tried, I couldn't even like her, let alone love her as Mom kept urging me to. It was hard to feel pity or anything but dislike for her.

It wasn't as if I hadn't tried. When Heather had first moved in, I'd done everything I could think of to be a good big sister, but she'd made it clear that she wanted nothing to do with me. If I tried to comb her hair, she pulled away, crying to Mom that I was hurting her. If I offered to read to her, she'd yawn after the first sentence or two and say the story was boring and dumb. Once I made the mistake of letting her play with my old Barbie dolls, the ones I was saving for my children; she cut their hair off playing beauty parlor and ripped their best outfits. She even tore up a family of paper dolls I made for her, taking great pleasure in beheading them right in front of me. Then she dropped them disdainfully in the trash can and walked out of the room.

To make it even worse, she told lies about Michael and me, making it sound as if we tormented her whenever we were alone with her. Dave believed her most of the time, and sometimes Mom did too. In the six months that Mom and Dave had been married, things had gotten very tense in our home, and, as far as I could see, Heather was responsible for most of the bad feelings. And now we were moving to a little church in the country where there would be no escape from her all summer. Was it any wonder that I was depressed?

I glanced at Michael, still hard at work on his math. My own poem was now almost obscured by the cats I'd drawn all over the notebook paper. I stared at it sadly, no longer in the mood to continue writing about unicorns, rainbows, and castles in the clouds. Tearing it out of my notebook, I crumpled it into a ball and tossed it at Speed Racer as he zipped past in his little car. Then I began writing a poem about real life. Something depressing dealing with loneliness and unhappiness and the misery of being misunderstood and unloved.

2

ON THE FIRST DAY of summer vacation, Dave and a bunch of his friends loaded everything we owned into a U-Haul truck and headed toward our new home in Holwell, Maryland. Dave drove the truck with Heather sitting beside him, looking very pleased with herself, and Mom, Michael, and I followed in our old van. Behind us was another van in even worse shape than ours, filled with Dave's friends.

After we turned off the Beltway, the roads narrowed and wound up and down hills, curved past farms, tunneled through forests. As we bounced along over ruts and bumps, Mom pointed out the scenic spots. "See that old barn over there?" she'd exclaim, pointing to a building on the verge of collapse. "Isn't that a perfect subject for a painting?"

When Michael and I mumbled something

about Andrew Wyeth having already painted a hundred barns just like it, she'd spot something else — a twisted old tree, a line hung with flapping clothes, a flock of geese strutting across a yard — and get excited all over again. "You two are just going to love living here," she said more than once, never losing hope that we'd eventually agree with her.

After a couple of hours of driving, Mom turned to us and said, "Here we are!" Swinging off the road behind the U-Haul, she pointed at the little white church. "Isn't it beautiful?"

It *was* pretty. No matter how much I preferred our row house, I had to admit that Mom and Dave had picked a lovely place. Quiet and peaceful, the small building sat by the side of the road, shaded by two huge maple trees. Although it had no steeple, the tall, pointed windows and red double doors left no doubt that it was indeed a church. On one side was an addition, built to harmonize with the original building, and on the other was the carriage house Dave planned to use as his pottery workshop.

Behind it rose a forest in deep green leaf, and, on either side, fields of corn basked in the morning sun. Across the road, a herd of cows gazed at us, their big brown eyes taking in everything.

"Look, it's the welcome wagon." Michael nudged me and pointed at the cows.

"Where are the other houses?" I looked around, hoping I'd missed seeing them.

"There's a farmhouse about a mile down the road," Mom said.

"But I thought we were moving to Holwell." I frowned at Mom.

"That's our post office address," she said, looking at herself in the rearview mirror and smoothing her hair. I could tell she was a little uncomfortable at having misled me deliberately or accidentally into thinking we would at least have neighbors and the prospect of making new friends. "The town itself is only a couple of miles away," she added apologetically.

"You said there was a library," Michael said, leaning across me, his voice full of anger. "I thought you meant it was just a few blocks away or something."

"You can ride your bikes into Holwell. It's not far." Mom opened her door and prepared to get out. "I told you we were moving to the country."

Before we could say anything else, Dave's friends pulled into the driveway behind us and screeched to a stop in a cloud of white dust. At the same time, Dave and Heather got out of the U-Haul and walked toward us. I couldn't help noticing that Dave looked a little tense and Heather was dragging on his hand, trying to keep him from joining Mom. Our first day in Holwell wasn't beginning very well.

"Come on, Jean," Dave said to Mom. "Let's get this show on the road."

"I'll carry my stuff in," Michael said, jumping out of the van. I knew he was worried that somebody would drop his insect collection or misplace his books.

"How about you taking care of Heather?" Dave tugged her toward me, despite her efforts to dig her heels into the dust. As usual, she was frowning through the tangles of hair almost hiding her face.

"What should I do?" I turned to Mom, hoping she'd suggest I help her with something important, but she sided with Dave as usual.

"You could take her for a walk," Mom said, patting my shoulder. "There's a nice, little path down through the woods." She pointed off to the right of the church. "It leads to a creek. You could wade or something."

"Don't go too far, though," Dave added, prying his fingers away from Heather's clutch.

Knowing I had no choice, I tried to take Heather's other hand, but she snatched it away, scowling at me as if I'd tried to pinch her.

"Go with Molly, now." Dave succeeded in freeing himself. "Daddy has a lot of work to do, honey. You and Molly can have a real nice time."

"I don't want to go with her," Heather whined, her voice rising in pitch. "I want to stay with you, Daddy. I don't like it here."

"You heard me, Heather. Don't make Daddy cross with you."

"Come on, Heather." I started walking toward the path, and, after some more pleading from Dave, she finally followed me. Silently we entered the cool shade of the trees. Above our heads, the leaves rustled softly and the sunlight splattered down through the branches, gleaming here and there at the whim of the wind. A butterfly as big as my hand fluttered across the path, and I was glad that Michael wasn't there. If he'd seen it, he'd have gotten his net and added it to his collection.

"Look, Heather." I pointed at the butterfly as it rested for a moment on a leaf. "Isn't it pretty?"

She glanced at it. "It's nothing but a caterpillar with wings," she muttered.

After that, I didn't try talking to her until we found the creek. The water was shallow, maybe two or three inches deep, and it was racing along over a bed of stones between low banks. It was perfect for wading. Sitting down, I took off my running shoes and socks.

"Want to come with me?" I asked her as I stepped out into the clear water.

She shook her head and continued following

the path along the creek. Shrugging my shoulders, I splashed along beside her, enjoying the feel of the cold water as it rose higher, creeping up to my knees as the creek narrowed and the banks grew steeper.

After wading for about five minutes, I came around a curve and was confronted with a rusty, barbed-wire fence from which hung a No Trespassing sign. On the other side, a herd of cattle looked up from the water and lowed. For a minute, I thought they were going to charge at me, fence or no fence, and I scrambled up the bank to Heather's side.

"They're just *cows*," she said, as if she knew I was thinking that they might be bulls. "They won't hurt you."

"I know," I said, trying to sound a lot more convincing than I felt. "Do you want to go back to the church?"

She gave me one of her disdainful looks. "Well, we can't go any farther, can we?" She looked pointedly at the fence and the cows watching us from the other side.

Still carrying my shoes, I followed Heather back down the path. Instead of turning off through the woods, taking the route we'd originally chosen, we walked farther along the creek. It was a pleasant path, cool and shady, and I was too busy watching a couple of dragonflies darting back and forth across the water to pay much attention to what Heather was doing. When she stopped suddenly just ahead of me, I bumped right into her.

"What's the matter?" I asked.

She looked at me over her shoulder. "Look." She pointed at a crooked fence almost hidden by weeds and bushes. "What's that?"

Despite the warmth of the afternoon, I felt goose bumps prick up all over me. "It's a graveyard," I whispered.

It wasn't very big, and the grass had grown almost as tall as the tombstones, but here and there a stone angel lifted its marble wings toward the sky, and a cross or two tilted out of the weeds. It was without a doubt the spookiest place I'd ever seen, and I wanted to run back to the church, but Heather stared at it, fascinated.

"Are you afraid?" she asked, her thumb hovering near her mouth.

"Of course not," I lied, reluctant to expose any weaknesses to Heather. Edging back down the path toward the church, I said, "Let's go see what Mom and Dave are doing. They're probably wondering where we are."

"It would be shorter to cut through the graveyard," Heather said, her pale eyes probing mine.

"It's probably private property," I said. "You could get in trouble for trespassing."

But Heather only smiled and slipped through a gap in the fence. "Come on, Molly," she said, daring me to follow her.

While I watched, she ran through the weeds, paying no attention to the tombstones. "It's bad luck to step on a grave," I called after her.

Pausing by a stone cherub, she caressed his cheek and then whirled about, performing a weird little dance as she wove in and out of the tombstones. "Molly is afraid," she chanted, "Molly is afraid."

"You're crazy!" I shouted at her. Then I turned my back on the graveyard and ran through the woods, ducking branches that reached for my hair and stumbling over roots. By the time I got to the church, I was out of breath and my heart was pounding so hard I thought my ribs would split. Catching sight of Mom disappearing through a side door, I followed her inside and caught up with her in the hall. I grabbed her arm and almost made her drop the box she was carrying.

"Molly, what's wrong?" She put the box down and stared at me. "Where is Heather? Has something happened?"

I shook my head, still gasping for breath. "There's a graveyard behind the church," I panted. "A graveyard!"

"Of course there is. It's part of the property."

"It's ours? We own a *graveyard*?"

"No, not exactly." Mom frowned at me. "For heaven's sake, Molly, have you run in here and scared me half to death just because of a graveyard?"

"You never said anything about it. You never told me we were going to have a bunch of dead people buried in our backyard." I started crying then, and Mom put her arm around me.

"Dead people in our yard?" Michael ran out of a room down the hall. "What's she talking about, Mom?"

"You found the graveyard." Dave appeared behind Michael, grinning as if I had done something marvelously clever.

"Why didn't you tell us?" I pulled away from Mom, wiping my eyes on my shirt tail. I didn't want Dave to know what a baby I was.

"I didn't think it was worth mentioning." Dave winked at Mom. "Just think what quiet neighbors they'll be. No wild parties, no loud music, no dropping in to borrow a cup of sugar or the lawn mower. Why, I bet they won't even speak to us." He gave Mom a hug and a kiss, and they both laughed while I stood there feeling foolish.

"Are the graves old?" Michael tried to push between Mom and me in his haste to go see them.

"Hey, hold it," Dave said, stopping him. "You're not finished getting your room in order, and Molly hasn't even started. You two get to work. You can see the graveyard later."

"That's not fair!" Michael said. "Molly's been playing with Heather ever since we got here, and I've been working. Can't I go outside for just a minute?"

"Where is Heather?" Dave asked as if he'd just realized she wasn't with me.

"The last time I saw her she was dancing around the graveyard," I said. "For all I know, she's still there." Without looking at him or Mom, I followed Michael down the hall to the room I had to share with Heather. As I shut the door behind me, I heard Heather come into the house.

"Molly ran away from me," she whined, her shrill voice carrying right through the closed door.

Heaving a great sigh, I prepared myself for a lecture from Dave and set about unpacking my books and arranging them on the shelves next to my bed. It was a nice room, I thought, bigger and airier than my old room in Baltimore, and, if I hadn't had to share it with Heather, I would have really enjoyed living in it.

From the window between our beds, I could see the mountains, but when I moved closer to see the whole view, I realized that the graveyard was only a short distance away, partially hidden from the house by a tall boxwood hedge. Shivering, I drew back from the window. How was I going to sleep at night, knowing how close it was?

3

THAT EVENING, after Dave's friends left, we had our first dinner in the church. Mom and Dave did most of the talking; they didn't make much of an effort to involve us in the plans they were making for their art projects. While they chattered about craft fairs and galleries, Heather picked at her food as if she expected to find crushed glass or rat poison hidden in it, and Michael described the huge centipede he'd caught in his bedroom, ignoring my pleas for him to talk about something less disgusting. How can a person enjoy eating spaghetti when her brother is babbling about a hideous, million-legged creature over four inches long?

As we were finishing our dessert, Mom suggested going for a walk before it got dark. Naturally, Michael suggested a tour of the graveyard, and everyone but me agreed. As they got ready to leave, I considered staying home and washing the dishes, but then I decided it might be worse to be all alone in the house. Reluctantly I followed them out the back door and down the brick path to the graveyard.

The sun was hovering on the mountaintops, and a tall oak tree at one end of the graveyard sent a long shadow over the grass toward us. As we entered the gate, a flock of crows rose from the oak and flew away, cawing loudly, as if we were trespassers. When I took Mom's hand, Heather smiled mockingly at me from her perch on Dave's shoulders.

"Molly's scared of the graveyard," she whispered in his ear, "but I'm not."

To prove how brave she was, she slipped down and ran ahead of us. Scrambling up on a tombstone, she spread her arms. "Look at me, Daddy," she called, "I'm an angel."

"Hey, get down from there." Dave grabbed her. "These are too old for you to climb on, honey. They could topple right over."

"I was just playing." Heather tugged at his beard, trying to braid it around her fingers. "At least I'm not a scaredy-cat."

While Dave was occupied with Heather, Mom turned to me and put her arm around my shoulders. "See how peaceful it is, Molly? There's nothing frightening about an old graveyard." She hugged me close.

I didn't say anything, nor did I try to pull away. Instead I snuggled closer, feeling safe as long I could feel her warm body next to mine.

"What's the matter, Molly?" Dave smiled at me over Heather's dark head. "Do you expect to see a ghost?"

Embarrassed, I forced myself to laugh. "Of course not. I'm just cold, that's all." And it was true. The sun had slipped down behind the mountains, taking the warmth of the day with it. A little breeze brought the chill of night with it as it tossed the heads of the Queen Anne's lace blooming all around us.

"Look," Michael called to us from the other side of the graveyard. "A whole family named Berry is buried here." He waved his arm at a cluster of tombstones guarded by a solemn marble angel. "This must be the Berry Patch!"

Everybody laughed at his joke but me. It didn't seem right to call out the names of dead people, especially if you were laughing. Uneasily, I followed Mom toward the angel, but I wanted very badly to go back to the church.

"Listen to this," Michael said. " 'Ada Berry, Beloved Wife of Edward Berry. April 3, 1811– November 28, 1899. Not Dead, Only Resting from Life's Weary Toil.' And here's her daughter, see? 'Susannah Berry, June 10, 1832–December 30, 1835. A Little Lamb in the Hands of the Lord.' And over here —"

"Oh, stop, Michael, stop." Mom pulled him away from the tombstone of another Berry child. "That's too sad. Don't read any more."

"I thought this was such a peaceful place," I murmured.

"Well, it is." Mom's voice wavered, though, and she looked past me at the sky where the first stars were beginning to glow.

"But don't you want to know how they died?" Michael asked. "Little kids like these probably died from smallpox or diphtheria or even measles. And this one right here, Adam Berry, died in 1863, and he was twenty-one. He was probably killed in the Civil War. A Yankee soldier, think of that."

"It's getting dark," I said, pointing out the obvious. "Why don't we go back to the church?"

"Yes," Mom agreed. "The mosquitoes have found me."

"Where has Heather run off to?" Dave scanned the graveyard, growing so dark now that everything was gray and indistinct.

"There she is." Michael pointed to the far end of the graveyard where the oak tree stood. In the shadows, we could barely see Heather poking around in the weeds.

"Come on, Heather," Dave called. "You'[ve]
all day tomorrow to explore this place. N[o]
these folks is going anywhere."

He and Mom chuckled, and he put his arm
around her waist and whispered something in
her ear that made her giggle. Glancing at Heather,
I saw her stop and stare at Dave and Mom. Even
in the darkness I could see the look of hatred
that flashed across her pale face at the sight of
him embracing Mom. Then, realizing that I was
looking at her, she made her face blank and
walked slowly toward us, trailing her fingers
across the tombstones and humming softly.

By the time we reached the church, the trees
were dark masses against the sky, flickering with
fireflies, and above us the sky was studded with
stars and a crescent moon barely clearing the oak
tree.

"Look at that." Mom paused on the back steps,
her head tilted back. "I'd forgotten how many
more stars you can see when you get away from
the city."

"There's the Milky Way and the Big Dipper,"
Michael said, "and the Little Dipper too."

"And the North Star." Dave pointed at something that only he could see. "If you're interested, Michael, I've got some astronomy books
we can look at."

While Mom and I washed the dinner dishes,

Dave got out a book and sat down at the kitchen table to explain one of the star charts to Michael. Finding herself with nothing to do, Heather climbed into Dave's lap and did all she could to make it impossible for him to talk to Michael.

"I'm sleepy, Daddy," she whispered. "I want you to put me to bed."

"Is your room all ready?" Dave asked.

"Yes, but I don't want to sleep there." She peeked at me, then tugged at Dave's beard.

"Why not, honey?" he asked, gently freeing his beard.

"Because of her." Heather looked at me again and snuggled closer to Dave. "I don't want to sleep with her."

Mom and Dave looked at each other and sighed as if they'd been expecting something of this sort. "Molly's your sister now, Heather," Dave said patiently. "Sisters always share."

Heather stuck out her lip and managed to squeeze a few tears out of her big, sad eyes. "She's mean to me."

"Oh, Heather," Mom said softly. "Molly's not mean to you."

When Mom tried to touch Heather's shoulder, she jerked away as if Mom had intended to hurt her. "You leave me alone!" Heather cried. "You're mean too, and I hate you both. Him too!"

She glared at Michael, then turned to Dave. "I don't want to live here with them. I want my own mother back!"

There was a little silence in the kitchen which made all the night noises — the crickets and the frogs, the wind in the leaves — seem louder.

"Now, now, honey." Dave stood up with Heather in his arms. "Daddy will tuck you in and tell you a little princess story. Wouldn't you like that?"

Heather buried her face in his neck, but as he carried her out the door, she looked at me and stuck out her tongue.

"Just ignore her, Molly," Mom said softly. "It's been a long day, and we're all tired."

"You always make excuses for her, no matter what she says or does." I flopped down in a chair beside Michael. "She's spoiled rotten."

"Oh, Molly, can't you be more understanding?" Mom looked at me sadly. "She's such an unhappy little girl."

"That doesn't give her the right to make us miserable too. The only thing that would make her happy is for you and Dave to split up. Can't you see that's what she wants?"

Mom shook her head. "That's a terrible thing to say, Molly. I'm ashamed of you."

"Molly's right," Michael said. "Heather hates

us. She's never going to be happy living here."

"If we give her enough love, she'll change," Mom said. "I know she will."

Michael and I looked at each other and shook our heads. Why couldn't Mom face facts?

"You two could try a little harder," Mom added in a crosser voice. "You've never really given her a chance. Always running away from her, teasing her, making her cry."

"Mom, that's not fair!" I jumped to my feet, ready to run to my room. "I've tried and tried and tried! But she twists everything I do all around and lies and then you believe her, not me!"

Mom turned her back and leaned on the sink. "Just try harder, Molly. Please?" She kept her face hidden as she spoke, and I realized that she was crying.

Running to her side, I put my arms around her and hugged her tightly, pressing my face into the little hollow beneath her collarbone. "Okay, Mom," I whispered, trying hard not to cry myself, "I'll try some more."

Mom hugged me fiercely. "I'm sorry, Molly. I know you've tried. I'm just so discouraged. I thought by now Heather would be happier with us, but sometimes I'm afraid you and Michael are right. She doesn't want my love." She wiped her tears away with the back of her hand and sighed. "I don't know what to do. I love Dave so much. And you all too. But Heather, I just don't know."

She made herself a cup of peppermint tea and carried it out on the back porch. Knowing she wanted to be alone, I sat down beside Michael. While he studied the star chart, I thought about Mom. I hated to see her so unhappy, but I had no idea what I could do to help her feel better. Heather sat in the middle of everything, making all of us miserable, and, as far as I could see, enjoying every minute of it.

4

---+---

WHILE MOM was still out on the porch, Dave came into the kitchen. Ruffling his hair with one hand, he sighed. "Well, Heather's asleep," he said, "so you two can get along to bed now yourselves. Don't wake her up, Molly. I've just about run out of little princess stories."

As Michael and I started to leave the room, Dave asked where Mom was.

"On the porch having a cup of tea," I said, as I followed Michael down the hall. Behind me, I heard the screen door open and shut and then Dave's voice murmuring something to Mom.

Pausing in his doorway, Michael said, "Want to come in and talk for a while, Molly?"

"Sure. I'm not in any hurry to go in there and take the chance of waking her up."

Michael's room already looked like home. His

framed insect displays were hanging on the wall over his bed; his aquarium was set up near the window, and his scientific apparatus — microscope, magnifying glass, butterfly net, and chemistry set — was in place on the long desk Dave had made for him. Books filled his shelves, mostly plant, bird, rock, and animal nature guides with a few Encyclopedia Browns, Hardy Boys, and Alfred Hitchcocks for variety.

Picking up one of his fossils, I examined the print of a tiny skeleton embedded in its surface. "Doesn't the graveyard bother you at all?" I asked.

"I think it's great," he said. "I'm going to make it into an archeological project. I'll study all the graves, and then figure out what the people died of."

"You don't mean you're going to dig them up?" I stared at him, horrified.

"Of course not. That's against the law. What do you think I am? A body snatcher?" Michael grinned and polished his glasses on his tee shirt. "Not that it wouldn't interest me. In fact, I wish I could. They dig up Indian burial grounds and primitive Iron Age people, and they learn a lot from the things buried with them."

"That's awful." I thought of all the movies I'd seen on TV involving the opening of pyramids and the curses of mummies. "I'd be scared to disturb somebody's bones." I shuddered just thinking about how horrible it would be to discover a skeleton.

"You really are scared of the graveyard, aren't you?" Michael sounded curious.

"There's something about it, Michael." I gazed past his curly head at the window's dark rectangle, thinking of the tombstones behind the hedge, the tall weeds silvery in the starlight. It seemed to me that they waited there in the night for something, and I folded my arms tightly across my chest and tried to convince myself that I was being silly.

"Do you believe in ghosts?" Michael leaned toward me. All he needed was a pipe in his mouth to make him the perfect scientist.

I shrugged. "I don't know." As usual, his rational approach was embarrassing me. I felt silly answering his questions. Pretending to yawn, I edged toward the door. "I think I'll go to bed, Michael."

He nodded. "If you hear any funny noises or see a face at the window, just yell for me," he said as I started down the hall to Heather's and my room.

I glared at him, sure now that I wouldn't be able to sleep for fear of what might be creeping toward the church from the graveyard.

"Just kidding, Molly," he whispered as I paused, my hand on my doorknob. "The only weird thing you'll see tonight is Heather."

Ignoring him, I tiptoed into the room. Except for the moonlight shining dimly through the window, it was dark, and I moved cautiously, not wanting to trip over anything and risk waking Heather. Pulling my pajamas out from under my pillow, I undressed and got into bed. I was anxious to fall asleep as quickly as possible so I wouldn't lie there thinking about horror movies and scary stories.

But you know how it is. The more you want to sleep the more you stay awake, hearing every strange sound and translating it into footsteps in the hall, bony hands at the window, the moans of ghosts in the shrubbery. When I heard a sort of whimper, I stiffened in terror and prepared myself for the appearance of a hideous creature. Forcing myself at last to open my eyes, I saw nothing but Heather, her pale face almost hidden by her dark curls tumbling over the pillow. As I watched, she moaned again and tossed restlessly, mumbling something that sounded like "Mommy, Mommy."

Turning my back, I grabbed my cassette player and put the earphones on. Soon all I heard was the voice of Julie Harris reading one of Emily

Dickinson's poems, a good inspiration for the poetry I planned to write this summer.

I woke up to the sound of a mower droning away outside. The sun was shining, and Heather's bed was empty. Glancing at my watch, I saw that it was nine o'clock. Hoping that Michael hadn't already disappeared in quest of new insects to add to his collection, I dressed and ran down the hall to the kitchen.

I found Heather and Mom sitting at the table, finishing their breakfast. Dave was already in the carriage house setting up his pottery workshop, and Mom said Michael was in the graveyard talking to Mr. Simmons.

"Who's Mr. Simmons?" I asked, pouring milk on my cereal.

"He's the graveyard's caretaker. He comes once a month or so to mow the grass and tidy the place up." Mom sipped her coffee. "He's a nice old chap, about seventy or eighty years old, but he carries himself like a soldier."

Remembering the height of the weeds, I had a feeling that Mr. Simmons had been on a vacation or something. "Maybe it won't look so gloomy after he finishes," I said.

Mom smiled and turned to Heather. "What would you like to do today, sweetie?" she asked.

Shoving her half-full bowl of cereal across the table, Heather got up and headed toward the back door.

"Where are you going?" Mom called after her.

The only answer she got was the sound of the screen door banging shut behind Heather.

"Oh, well, I guess she'll be all right outside." Mom went to the window over the sink and watched Heather amble across the lawn toward the hedge and the sound of the mower. "Poor Mr. Simmons. I guess she wants to see what he's up to."

She crossed the room and paused beside me. "I've got a lot to do, Molly. As soon as you finish eating, please go out and keep an eye on Heather. I don't want her wandering off."

"Can't I stay in and help you?"

She patted my shoulder. "The nicest thing you can do for me is to look after Heather."

Before I could say anything more, she left the room. Glumly I ate the rest of my cereal and went outside in search of Heather and Michael. By the time I got to the graveyard, Mr. Simmons had finished mowing. He was clipping and trimming the weeds around the tombstones, and Michael was raking the cut grass into a pile next to the wheelbarrow. Heather was sitting on a fallen tombstone trying clumsily to make a daisy chain. When she saw me hesitating at the gate, she said, "Molly's afraid to come in here. She thinks something's going to get her."

Mr. Simmons looked up and smiled at me. "Well, good morning, Molly. Won't you join us?"

Taking a deep breath, I walked toward him, careful, as usual, not to step on anybody's grave. Now that the grass was cut, it was easier to see where it was safe to walk. In fact, the whole place looked at lot less scary than it had before.

"Mr. Simmons says this is a real old graveyard," Michael told me. "The church was built way back in 1825, so some of the graves are 160 years old. Isn't that something? The Civil War hadn't even happened then. But nobody's been buried here since 1950. Isn't that right?" Michael turned to Mr. Simmons.

The old man nodded his head. "They filled the graveyard up, that's what they did. Old Mrs. Perkins was the last one to get in." He pointed at a pink stone with a shiny front. "Right there she is. My first-grade teacher." He grinned and shook his head. "She's not handing out any more report cards now, is she?"

Michael laughed, but I felt sad just thinking about Mrs. Perkins. "Caroline," it said on the stone. "Dear, Departed Wife of John Albert Perkins. She will long be missed."

"And right over here," Mr. Simmons went on,

"is where my mother and father are sleeping."
He rested his old hands on two stones. "I brought
flowers for them and my baby sister, too."

I looked at the mason jars full of wild flowers
decorating the three graves. "They look very
pretty," I said, wondering if he felt sad. "It must
be awful when a baby dies," I added, staring at
the tiny headstone marking his sister's grave.

"They didn't have the medicine then, you
know," he said. "Measles, chicken pox, whoop-
ing cough, scarlet fever, that's what killed the
children."

As Michael nodded, glad that Mr. Simmons
was backing up his own theories, Heather joined
us. "Fire too," she said. "Lots of people died in
fires, didn't they?"

Mr. Simmons looked a little surprised. "They
did indeed," he said.

"My mother died in a fire." Heather dropped
a dandelion on the baby's grave and walked away.

Mr. Simmons watched her for a moment, then
turned to us. "I thought she was your sister," he
said.

"No, her father married our mother." Michael
nudged the dandelion away from the baby's grave
with his bare toe. "She's our stepsister."

"Her mother died in a fire?" Mr. Simmons
asked.

"When Heather was three. They were all alone

in the house, and Heather almost died too. She was unconscious when the rescue squad found her," I told him.

"Poor little thing," he said sympathetically. Turning away, he returned to his work, clipping carefully around each stone and whistling. The sweet smell of cut grass drying in the hot sun filled the air, mingling with the aroma of Mr. Simmons' pipe. A mockingbird perched on a tombstone and sang; butterflies flashed about, and for a while I forgot my fears and helped Michael scoop the grass cuttings into the wheelbarrow.

"You haven't mowed under the tree," I heard Heather say suddenly. She was frowning at Mr. Simmons' back as he knelt at the base of the Berrys' marble angel.

He squinted up at her. "Not enough grass under that old tree to bother with," he said pleasantly.

"There's weeds though."

"I just tend to the tombstones." Mr. Simmons returned his attention to the grass, but Heather didn't take the hint.

"But there's a grave there," she said, her lip jutting out. "I saw it."

Mr. Simmons straightened up and stared at her. "Couldn't be. Too many roots to bury somebody there."

"The tombstone is lying down in the weeds,"
Heather insisted. "Come with me. I'll show you."
She started walking toward the dense shade under the oak tree, and Mr. Simmons shrugged and
followed her.

Michael turned to me. "Aren't you coming
with us, Molly?"

I started to go with them, but I felt my goose
bumps coming back. The cheerfulness of the day
was gone, as surely as if a cloud had covered the
sun. Something was wrong; I could sense it if no
one else could. Staying where I was, next to the
relative safety of Mrs. Perkins' shiny new tombstone, I watched the three of them step into the
oak tree's shadow. Heather pointed at something in the grass, and Mr. Simmons bent down
to get a better look.

"Looks like you're right," I heard him say to
Heather.

"Come here, Molly!" Michael called. "This is
really interesting."

As Heather smiled at me over her shoulder,
daring me as she had before, I forced myself to
join them. Mr. Simmons was struggling to right
a small, weather-stained stone. "Well, I'll be,"
he said. "I've been tending these graves for
twenty-some years, and I never knew this one
was here. Never even looked for it."

With the stone erect, he scraped away the dirt

and moss to reveal the inscription. " 'H.E.H,' " he read out loud, tracing the letters with his fingers. " 'March 7, 1879—August 8, 1886. May she rest in peace.' " He shook his head and set to work pulling out the weeds growing around the base of the stone. "Strange, isn't it?"

"Why is it strange?" Michael asked.

"Well, she was just a child. Seven years old. Where's the rest of the family?"

"What do you mean?" Michael squatted beside him, staring at the gravestone.

"Well, look around, son. Families get buried together," he said.

"That's right. Like the Berry Patch." Michael nodded astutely.

Mr. Simmons looked puzzled for a moment, but then he chuckled. "Yes, yes, the Berry Family. All together they are with their very own angel to watch over them." He relit his pipe and stood up, gazing about the graveyard.

"The stones usually say 'Beloved Daughter of ' or something like that," he mused, "but here's this child, all by herself. No name. Just the initials. No other grave close by. It just doesn't seem right somehow."

"It's my initials," Heather said suddenly, removing her thumb from her mouth and touching the stone lightly. "Heather Elizabeth Hill."

"My age too," she added as we all stared at her.

"Well, now, that is a coincidence," Mr. Simmons said. Lopping away the last of the weeds, he took Heather's hand and led her out into the sunlight. "I wouldn't play here," he said to her. "Even with the weeds gone, it's a good place for snakes. Poison ivy, too, from the looks of it." He gestured at the shiny green leaves flourishing in the shade and twisting up the oak's trunk.

"I'm not afraid of snakes," Heather said. "Or poison ivy either. I never get it."

Mr. Simmons frowned down at her. "You listen to what I tell you, young lady. That's the kind of shade a copperhead loves. One of them bites you, you'll know it."

Heather gave the old man a scornful look and pulled away from him. "I'll play wherever I want to. You're not my boss." Then she stalked off, head high, black curls lifting in the breeze.

"Uppity little creature," Mr. Simmons said. "How about giving me a hand with the wheelbarrow?" he asked Michael.

As the two of them trundled off toward the compost heap, I walked back to the house. Although Heather was nowhere in sight, I could hear Dave's voice in the carriage house, and I supposed she'd gone in there to tell him how mean Mr. Simmons was.

Finding a shady spot on the back steps, I sat down and gazed across the yard at the oak tree standing guard over H.E.H.'s lonely grave. Why hadn't the child's name been carved on the tombstone? Why was it all alone? I shivered again, despite the heat, and wondered how I would feel if the initials had been mine instead of Heather's.

5

———— ✦ ————

AFTER LUNCH, Mom sent Heather and me to our room to finish unpacking. "I want every box emptied and all your things put where they belong," she insisted as Heather started to whine in protest. "If you're having trouble finding places for everything," Mom added, "ask Molly to help you. That's what big sisters are for."

Without saying another word, Heather began unpacking, stuffing clothes into her bureau and books and toys onto the shelves on her side of the room. Ignoring the mess she was making, I concentrated on arranging my books and papers as neatly as possible. At least my side would look nice.

After a while, Heather lay down on her bed and shut her eyes. Thinking she'd gone to sleep, I finished putting my clothes into my bureau and lay down on my bed to read. I was so absorbed in *Watership Down* that I jumped when Heather suddenly spoke to me.

"What do you think that child's name is?" She was still lying down, gazing up at the ceiling where the leaves of the maple cast ever-shifting patterns. "Do you think it could be Heather Elizabeth Hill?"

"Of course not. That's *your* name."

"Suppose the initials were M.A.C?" Heather whispered.

"Those are my initials." I frowned at her.

"Would you be scared?"

I shrugged. "Not especially. Why? Are you scared?"

She sat up and shook her head. "No. I think it's interesting, that's all." She smiled at me. "But you would be scared, Molly. I know you'd be. You're afraid right now, and they aren't even your initials."

"Don't be silly." I opened my book again. "If you're finished asking questions, I'd like to get back to my reading."

"That's a dumb story," Heather said, getting up and staring out the window. "I hate rabbits. Who cares what happens to them?"

Ignoring her, I concentrated hard on Fiver's desperate attempts to warn the rabbits that danger was coming. This was the second time I'd read the book, and Fiver was my favorite character. I knew I would enjoy the story more this time, knowing that he was going to be all right.

Heather didn't say anything more. When I glanced at her to see what she was doing, she was still standing at the window gazing out at the graveyard as silently as a marble angel contemplating eternity.

As the days passed, the five of us got caught up in our own routines. From morning until night, Dave worked at the pottery wheel in the carriage house, throwing bowls, plates, mugs, pitchers, and jugs, mixing glazes, and tending his kiln, trying to get ready for a big August Craft Show. Although he didn't seem to mind our coming in and out, watching him work, he wasn't particularly interested in what we were doing. As long as we turned up for meals and bedtime, he didn't worry about us.

Mom was just as bad. She was terribly excited about having a real studio after so many years of setting up her easel in the corner of the kitchen or the bedroom, wherever she could find some unwanted space. She was working on a large painting of a barn. The colors were soft and muted, and all the edges were hazy as if the morning sun hadn't quite broken through the fog. You could almost smell the damp boards when you looked at it.

But Mom didn't like to be watched while she was painting; it ruined her concentration and made her self-conscious. So she'd always tell me to go outside and play. I guess she felt that we were all safe out here in the country. The things she worried about in Baltimore — drug dealers, child molesters, speeding cars — didn't exist in Holwell. The only thing she ever asked me to do was to keep an eye on Heather. She thought both Michael and I, being older, should take care of her.

Of course, that was the one thing neither of us did. Every morning, as soon as Dave disappeared into the carriage house and Mom went to her loft, Michael grabbed his butterfly net and kill jar and ran to the woods in pursuit of insects to add to his collection. Although I could have gone with him (and sometimes did), I usually took a book and my journal and wandered off somewhere to read or write.

And Heather? For a long time I had no idea where she went or how she spent her time. She might start out on the couch next to me, coloring or reading or watching television. Then, without my actually noticing, she'd disappear. She reminded me of a cat I used to own; one minute he'd be curled up next to me, and the next minute he'd be gone without making a sound.

One hot afternoon, I went outside looking for something to do. The air was hot and heavy with humidity, and I decided to walk down by the creek, maybe wade or something, just to cool off. Leaving my book on the bank, I splashed through the water without realizing how close I was getting to the graveyard. When I looked up and saw the tombstones above me, I hesitated, thinking I'd turn back in the direction of the cows.

Then I heard a voice. Was it Heather's? The breeze swirled the leaves, the creek chattered over stones, birds sang, insects chirped and buzzed, making it impossible to be sure who was speaking. Uneasily, I climbed the bank and tiptoed down the path beside the graveyard.

I found Heather sitting in the shade staring at the small tombstone under the oak tree. On the grave, she had placed a peanut butter jar filled with black-eyed Susans and Queen Anne's lace. As I watched, scarcely daring to breathe, she said something in a voice too low for me to hear, her hands flashing in the shadows as she gestured nervously.

Then she sat back, her mouth half-open, her eyes half-closed, nodding her head as if she were in a trance. All around me the leaves rustled, and I shivered, sure that the noise they made was hiding words from me that were audible to Heather. Convinced that she was in danger, I leaned toward her, peering through a tangle of honeysuckle, wondering what I should do.

"Oh, Helen," Heather said suddenly, her voice louder. "Will you really be my friend? I'll do anything you say — I promise I will — if you'll be my friend."

Again she was silent, her head tilted to one side, a smile twitching the corners of her mouth. The breeze blew again, making a dry sound, a whispering, and Heather nodded. "I'll wait for you, Helen. When you come, I'll be the best friend you ever had, cross my heart."

As she leaned forward to rearrange the flowers, I gripped the fence and called to her. "What are you doing, Heather? Who are you talking to?"

She leaped to her feet, her face pale and angry. "Molly!" she screamed, "Go away! Go away!"

"Not until you tell me what you're doing!" I shivered as the breeze gusted through the honeysuckle, filling the air with sweetness. Something hung in the space between us. For a moment, I felt it watching me. Then it was gone, and all around me the insects struck up a chorus of cheerful summer sounds.

"I don't have to tell you anything." Heather's

narrow face was almost expressionless, mask-like, as if it hid secrets, terrible secrets.

"You were talking to someone. I *heard* you. You called her Helen."

Without looking at me, Heather took a flower from the jar. Pulling a petal off, she dropped it and watched it flutter down to the grave. "You didn't *see* anybody. Or even hear anybody, did you?" She glanced at me, her tangled hair almost hiding her eyes.

"There was something," I insisted. "I know there was."

Heather shook her head and continued pulling the petals off, one by one. She watched them as they drifted with the breeze down to the earth. "Don't spy on me anymore, Molly," she said softly. "I don't like to be spied on."

"You better come out from under that tree," I yelled. "You heard what Mr. Simmons said about snakes and poison ivy."

"I'll stay here as long as I want." Heather finished stripping the flower of its petals and bent to pick up another one. "If you want me, you'll have to come here and get me," she said.

A ray of sunlight lanced down through the oak's leaves and touched the jar of flowers, and from somewhere in the branches overhead a crow cawed. Folding my arms tightly across my chest, I backed away from the graveyard. "Get bitten by a snake," I said as I began walking back toward the church. "See if I care!"

The only answer was the rustling of leaves and a faint sound of laughter. Without looking back, I quickened my pace, anxious to get away from Heather and whatever else might be lingering under that tree.

Although I tried to tell Mom that I thought that the graveyard was haunted, she was too busy fixing dinner to listen to me. "Honestly, Molly," she said, "Reading all that poetry is making you morbid. Now get busy and put ice in the glasses so I can pour the tea."

"But, Mom, if you'd been there —" I started to say, but she looked so exasperated, I stopped in mid-sentence. What was the use?

After dinner, I found Michael out on the front porch watching the stars come out. "See that one, right there?" He pointed at a bright star hanging just above the mountains across the valley. "That's a planet. Venus. You can see it in the morning, too."

I nodded and sat down beside him, trying to think of a good way to introduce the subject of ghosts. "Do you believe in things you can't prove?" I asked him.

He looked at me as if he were a little puzzled. "Like what?"

"Oh, I don't know. Ghosts and stuff like that."
I hugged my knees against my chest and turned
my back to the graveyard.

Michael laughed. "What's the matter? Are you
still scared you'll see something looking in your
window at night?"

"Don't laugh, Michael." I glared at him. "I'm
not just kidding around." Glancing over my
shoulder to make sure Heather wasn't standing
behind us eavesdropping, I told him about her
strange behavior in the graveyard.

"So?" Michael swatted a mosquito on his arm.
"You know how she is, always living in some
weird little world of her own. She probably has
an imaginary friend, and you embarrassed her."

"You didn't see her, Michael. It wasn't just
her imagination. There was something there; I
could sense it." I took a deep breath. "It scared
me, Michael."

"Oh, Molly," Michael laughed, "next you'll
be telling me you actually saw a ghost."

"I told you not to laugh!" I yelled. "It's not
funny!"

"No, it's not funny. It's not funny at all."

Michael and I spun around. Heather was
standing just inside the screen door, her face
pressing against it. "There's nothing funny about
Helen," she added softly.

"Mom should get you a collar with bells on

it," Michael said, "like cats wear to warn birds. Then maybe you couldn't sneak up and spy on people."

"Molly spies on me," Heather hissed. "She spied on me and Helen today!"

"See?" I turned to Michael.

Before he could say anything, Heather looked at us, a frown creasing her face. "Molly's right. You better not laugh, Michael. Helen doesn't like either one of you, and when she comes, you'll be sorry for everything you ever did to me."

Without waiting for an answer, Heather turned away and disappeared into the shadows in the hall.

"There," I whispered, clutching Michael's arm. "Do you see what I mean?"

Michael pulled away from me. "Don't let that little brat scare you with make-believe, Molly. You're acting like a real dope."

"I am not!" Tears stung my eyes, and I ran into the house, almost colliding with Mom as she came out of the kitchen.

"I was just looking for you and Michael," she said cheerfully. "Would you like some ice cream? Heather and Dave and I were just about to sit down and try the ice-cream maker we got last week. How about it?"

Behind her, in the lighted kitchen, I could see Dave setting up the machine while Heather watched. He turned to her and said something, and she laughed and gave him a strawberry to sample.

"Now, Dave," Mom said, "I saw that! Don't eat them all, or we won't have enough for the ice cream."

"Daddy can have all he wants!" Heather stuck out her lip and scowled at Mom.

As Dave turned to Heather, I edged past Mom. "No, thanks," I said. "I'm not in the mood for ice cream."

"But, honey . . ." Mom started, reaching out to stop me.

I kept on going. "She ruins everything," I said to Mom before going in my room and shutting the door. I hoped Heather would stay in the kitchen until I was asleep.

6

THAT NIGHT, Heather had her first bad dream. She woke me up screaming, "Help, help, it's on fire! Put it out, Mommy, put it out!"

I jumped out of bed, switched on the light, and ran to her. She was sitting up in bed, her eyes squeezed shut, clutching her blanket. Tears ran down her cheeks, and she was trembling.

"Save me, save me!" she cried.

"Heather!" I grabbed her shoulders and shook her. "You're having a bad dream. Wake up!"

Michael stumbled into the room. "What's going on? What's wrong with her?"

Twisting and turning, Heather squirmed away from me and started running down the hall, still screaming about the fire. Dave caught her and picked her up. "It's all right, honey, it's all right," he murmured, rocking her as if she were a baby.

Suddenly she collapsed against him, perfectly relaxed. Her mouth found her thumb; her long eyelashes fluttered against her cheeks; her legs dangled like a rag doll's. Gently Dave carried her back into our room and lowered her into bed.

"There now," he whispered. Smoothing her hair back from her forehead, he kissed her.

Heather's eyes opened for a second, and she smiled at her father before sinking back into sleep.

Turning to me, Dave whispered, "What happened?"

"She was screaming about the fire. I tried to wake her up, but I couldn't. Then she jumped out of bed and ran out into the hall." I took Mom's hand and slid closer to her. Was he going to blame me somehow?

Dave shook his head and ran his hands through his hair, making it stand up in spikes. "She hasn't had those nightmares for so long; I thought she'd gotten over them." Looking at me again, he asked, "Did anything upset her today?"

"Well, she was in the graveyard," I said uneasily. "She was talking to someone. She thinks there's a girl there, Helen." It sounded so ridiculous when I talked about it that I was embarrassed. I already knew what Michael and Mom thought about ghosts; I was sure Dave would have the same reaction.

Just as I thought, Dave smiled. "Heather's very imaginative." He said it as if I'd criticized her. "And very sensitive. You and Michael haven't been asking her questions about the fire, have you?"

"Of course not!" I stared at him, shocked. Surely he knew that Michael and I had promised not to talk to Heather about the fire. Did he think we would go back on our word?

"I thought something might have stirred up her memories." He tugged on his beard, gazing at me as if he weren't sure I could be trusted to tell the truth.

"It's what happened in the graveyard," I said. "There's something bad under the oak tree; I know there is! You should make her stay away from it. Even Mr. Simmons told her not to go near it because of snakes and poison ivy."

"Snakes and poison ivy are one thing," Dave said slowly, "but don't you ever start scaring her with stories about 'bad' things in the graveyard."

"Molly thinks the graveyard's haunted," my loyal brother said. "She's sure some ghost is after Heather."

Mom and Dave both turned on me then. "That's the most ridiculous thing I've ever heard, Molly," Mom said, and Dave agreed.

"No more talk about ghosts," he said.

"Especially not around Heather. I don't want you scaring her. No wonder she had a nightmare."

"But I didn't tell *her*, she told *me!*" I pulled away from Mom, feeling betrayed first by Michael and then by her. "And, besides, you didn't see her, you didn't hear her!"

Michael laughed. "Molly didn't scare Heather," he said. "Heather scared Molly."

Dave sighed and put his arm around Mom's shoulders. "Well, no sense standing here all night arguing about it," he said. "Just don't inflict your own fears on Heather, Molly. You've been fretting about that graveyard ever since we moved in here. It doesn't bother anybody else, so forget it, okay?" He reached out and gave my head a pat.

As I started to go back into my room, he added, "I see Heather's visits to the graveyard as a way of coming to terms with her mother's death. It's probably good for her. As long as nobody scares her." He looked at me again, leaving no doubt about whom he meant.

Closing my door, I tiptoed back to bed. Before I lay down, I peeked at Heather. The moonlight shone on her face, and I was sure her eyes were open a tiny slit. "I bet you lay here and listened to every word we said," I whispered, but she didn't answer. Turning my back to her and the window, I switched on my tape player and fell asleep listening to *West Side Story*.

The next morning, after Dave had disappeared into the carriage house, Mom into her loft, and Michael into the woods, I sat at the breakfast table with Heather, watching her poke at the cereal in her bowl.

"What are you going to do today?" I asked her.

"Nothing." She carried her bowl to the garbage can and dumped most of her cereal.

"I bet you're going to the graveyard again."

She looked at me over her shoulder, tangles of hair almost hiding her face. "Maybe I am and maybe I'm not. It's none of your business, is it?"

"There isn't really a ghost, is there? You were making it all up."

"You heard what Daddy said last night. No more talk about ghosts or trying to scare me. I'm going to tell him you're still doing it." With her hand on the screen door, she added, "You better not follow me or spy on me either. You'll be sorry if you do. Helen doesn't like people who bother me."

Before I could say anything, she was gone, leaving the screen door to bang shut behind her. Running to the window over the sink, I watched her saunter across the yard and disappear through the graveyard gate. Just once, she looked back and scowled at me.

Since it was my day to wash the breakfast dishes, I filled the sink with hot, soapy water and watched the bowls and mugs and glasses slowly fill and sink beneath the bubbles. While I washed them, I wondered what I should do about Heather and the ghost. If there were a ghost. In the morning sunlight, it seemed almost likely that I had imagined the presence of something inhuman under the oak tree. Maybe Mom was right about the poetry I'd been reading. Especially the Poe.

After I finished the dishes, I made my bed, trying to ignore the tangle of sheets, blankets, and clothes on Heather's bed. Then I picked up *Watership Down* and went outside to read.

Stretching out in the shade of one of the maples, I opened my book, but the warmth of summer made it hard to concentrate. In the droning of bees, in the rustling of leaves, in the swaying of wild flowers, I imagined I heard Helen's voice whispering to Heather, calling her, promising her things. Closing my book, I left it under the tree and crossed the lawn to the graveyard. I crept along the outside of the hedge, paused when I reached the oak tree, and peered through the leaves at the little stone, expecting to see Heather sitting there. All I saw was the peanut butter jar, filled with fresh flowers.

Pushing through the hedge, I forced myself to approach the tombstone. "H.E.H," I read. "March 7, 1879–August 8, 1886." She had been dead for a hundred years, so much longer than she'd been alive. What was left of her now? A tangle of bones? Maybe nothing but dust. I shivered, cold in the shade of the oak, hugging myself to get warm.

Thinking about the snakes, I backed away from the grave, feeling the warm sunlight strike my back as I moved out of the shade of the oak. With bees droning in the Queen Anne's lace and a butterfly flitting around my head, it was strange to think of death, especially the death of a little girl, younger even than I was. Could she really still be here, haunting this grave? If she did exist, what did she want? A breeze sighed through the leaves of the oak. It was the loneliest sound I'd ever heard, as lonely as a ghost who had been lying alone in the dark for a hundred years.

Overwhelmed with a terrible feeling of sadness and despair, I turned and ran out of the graveyard, feeling my heart pound. I wanted to go to Mom, but I knew she would laugh at me, or worse, get cross. Knowing it was useless to turn to Dave, I decided to look for Michael. I guessed he was somewhere in the woods and followed the path along the creek, hoping I might find him trying to catch crawfish where the water slowed near the fence.

At the end of the path, though, all I saw were the cows, standing knee-deep in the creek and staring stupidly at me. As I looked around, wondering where Michael might have gone, I noticed a path on the other side of the creek, angling off into the trees. It looked like the sort of thing Michael would enjoy exploring, so I pulled off my sandals, waded across, and followed the path into the woods.

After walking for about ten minutes, I found myself beside the creek again. Ahead of me, the woods thinned out, and I saw a large pond. Hurrying toward it, I looked around for Michael, sure he'd be here, but there was no sign of him.

On the rising ground above the pond were the ruins of an old stone house. Although the wall was two stories high on the side facing the water, the rest of the house was a crumbling heap of rock and charred wood. Long ago it must have burned, I thought. But before that, it must have been beautiful, standing there on the hill looking out across the valley to the mountains.

While I was gazing at the house, trying to imagine it whole, I saw a flash of color, the red of a tee shirt instantly visible. Thinking it was Michael, I started to call him, then stopped myself. Heather had been wearing a red tee shirt when she ran out of the kitchen this morning. What was she doing here, so far away from home?

Running across the clearing between the house and the pond, I crept through the underbrush surrounding the ruins, trying hard to make no noise. As I reached the corner of the house, I heard Heather's voice and dropped silently to my knees. Crawling through a thicket of polk berries and honeysuckle, I spotted Heather sitting on what once must have been a terrace.

"It's lovely here, Helen," she said, turning toward a space in the air, a sort of shimmering emptiness that reminded me of heat waves thrown out by a camp fire on a hot day. I was sure that Heather could see someone or something, that she could hear a voice speaking in the breeze.

Shivering, I felt the hairs on my neck and arms rise. At any moment I expected to see what Heather saw, and I was sure that Michael would not laugh if he were here. Even Mom and Dave would have to believe me. Heather was not sitting on that stone bench alone talking to an imaginary friend. Something was with her, and I was sure it was no friend.

Very slowly and cautiously, I backed away into my tunnel through the underbrush. All of a sudden, the house seemed threatening, more frightening than the graveyard itself. Its ruined walls towered over me, smoke-scorched and smelling still of charred wood and ash. Something terrible had happened here — I knew it had — and I wanted to get away, to save myself from whatever waited here in its ruins.

Breaking free of the bushes and trees I ran toward the pond, not caring now whether Heather saw me or not. Once I reached the safety of the woods, I slowed down and finally collapsed on a fallen tree, gasping for breath.

While I sat there, trying to breathe normally, I heard someone coming down the path. Looking up, I saw Heather walking toward me. At the sight of me, she stopped, obviously startled.

"What are you doing here?" Her hands balled into fists, she stood in the middle of the path, sunlight and shadow mottling her face and clothes with random patches of darkness and light. "You followed me again!"

Standing up to give myself the advantage of height, I shook my head. "I was looking for Michael," I said, "and I saw you on the terrace, talking to someone."

Heather tilted her head to one side, her jaw protruding at a stubborn angle. "So?"

"Heather, this isn't a good place." Frightened, I reached out to take her arm, but she sidestepped me.

"Don't try to tell me what to do, Molly!" Heather's gray eyes stared into mine. "This is Helen's house; she invited me here, and I'll come whenever I want to! You're the one who better stay away."

"Listen to me, Heather, please. Helen isn't your friend. She, she — I don't know what she is, but she's dangerous. Stay away from her!" I seized the little girl's arms and shook her. "Don't come here anymore!"

As quickly as a cat, Heather wriggled away from me. "Since when did you ever care what I do? Helen's a better friend than you've been. She understands me, she likes me!" Heather's thin chest rose and fell rapidly as she backed off, her eyes huge and frightened in her pale face. "Don't you dare try to take her away from me!"

A shift in the breeze lifted the leaves over our heads, and a ray of sunlight struck Heather, glinting on a silver locket I'd never seen before. Aware of my eyes, Heather closed a small hand over the locket.

"What's that?" I moved toward her, but she turned and ran away from me, back toward the church.

"She gave it to me," Heather cried over her shoulder. "It's mine and you can't see it!"

I stood still for a moment and watched her vanish around a curve in the path, her thin white legs flashing through the weeds. Fearfully I glanced back at the ruins of the house on the hill. For a moment I thought I saw a face at one of the windows, but I wasn't sure. The honeysuckle and ivy draping the walls were fluttering in the breeze, and what I saw could have been a shadow or a patch of sunlight.

Without looking at the house again, I ran down the path after Heather.

7

WHEN I GOT BACK to the church, I found Mom in the kitchen making sandwiches for herself and Heather.

"You're just in time for lunch, Molly," Mom said, but Heather merely glanced at me before returning her attention to the peanut butter she was smearing on a slice of bread.

"I'm not very hungry." I leaned against the counter, not knowing whether I should stay or leave. Just being around Heather was beginning to make me nervous. "Where's Michael?" I asked Mom.

"I suppose he's out in the woods somewhere." Mom held a bowl of tuna salad toward me. "Sure you don't want some?"

I shook my head. "Maybe later."

Without looking at Mom or me, Heather took her sandwich and opened the screen door.

"Where are you going, Heather?" Mom asked.

"I'm eating with Daddy," she said, letting the door bang shut behind her.

Silently Mom and I watched her walk across the yard and disappear into the carriage house.

"Where were you all morning?" Mom asked me. "Were you with Heather?"

Opening the refrigerator, I made a pretence of looking for the ice tea. When I found it, I poured myself a glass and offered some to Mom, still trying to think of an answer that wouldn't get me into trouble.

"We were out in the woods," I said finally, hoping she would assume that we were together. "There's an old house way down the creek, just ruins really, and a pond. Heather loves going there, but I think it's kind of dangerous."

"What do you mean, Molly?" Mom looked puzzled. "I didn't know there were any old houses nearby."

"Well, it's there. And the pond might be very deep. Not only that, but the walls of the house look like they might fall down any minute. It's not a good place for a kid to play, Mom, and I think you or Dave should tell Heather not to go there."

Mom sipped her tea. "It doesn't sound very safe," she said, "but I'd love to see it. I might want to sketch it."

"But will you tell Heather she can't go there?"

"Of course." Mom gave me a long look. "You know, though, Molly, that Dave and I count on you and Michael to take care of Heather. It's up to you to make sure she doesn't run wild in the woods all day."

"I try to watch her, but she sneaks away from me the minute my back is turned. And Michael never even tries. He just packs up his binoculars and his other junk and disappears into the woods."

Mom carried her dishes to the sink and began rinsing them. "Molly, you are old enough to be responsible. We moved here so Dave and I would have time to work without worrying about you all." Putting her plate and glass on the counter to drain, she wiped her hands on the seat of her shorts and smiled at me. "Go on, now, and find something to do. I've got to get back to my painting."

"But I don't have anything to do!" I wailed.

"Go find Michael. He manages to keep himself very happy." With that, Mom was out the back door, across the drive, and into the church.

After spending a long, hot afternoon reading *Watership Down* and trying not to think about

Helen or the ruins of her house, I was glad to see Michael stroll out of the woods just before dinner. Marking my place with a blade of grass, I ran to meet him.

"Look at the walking-stick I caught!" Michael brandished a jar in front of my face, but all I could see in it was a dead stick. "Isn't he great?"

All of a sudden I realized that the stick had legs and eyes. Backing away, I yelled, "Don't let that thing loose in the house!"

"It won't hurt you." Michael smiled at the creature in the jar. "They're real hard to see, but this old guy moved just when I was looking at him. He's a great example of natural camouflage."

"Good for him." Walking beside the great naturalist, but not too close, I told him about the old house. "Heather says Helen used to live there, Michael. And she has this chain around her neck with a locket on it. She says Helen gave it to her. You should have heard Heather talking to her — I don't think she's making it up; I think Helen really is there. I swear I almost saw her!"

All the things I hadn't been able to tell Mom came tumbling out while Michael listened, his face blank. Finally he interrupted me.

"Molly, cut it out," he said. "You should hear yourself! You're letting that kid make a fool of you."

"I am not!" I glared at him, furious. "You weren't there; you didn't see Heather or hear her! You didn't see her in the graveyard either."

Michael held up his jar and peered at the walking-stick. "Show me the house," he said.

"It's too late now. Dinner's almost ready, and by the time we finish, it will be dark."

"Tomorrow morning then. First thing." He grinned at me through the jar. "I've always wanted to explore a haunted house. Just think, a treasure could be buried in the cellar or something."

"I'm not going inside, and I don't think you should either. The walls are about to fall down."

"You are a scaredy-cat, you know that?" Michael waved the jar at me, and I jumped away. "Bugs, graveyards, old houses — you're scared of everything."

Before I could come back with a good retort, Mom stepped out on the back porch. "Dinner's ready, you two," she called.

As usual, Mom and Dave did most of the talking, but as we were finishing our dessert, Dave turned to Heather and said, "I hear that you and Molly discovered an old house in the woods."

Heather shot me a nasty look and nodded her head. "I found it, not Molly," she mumbled, her mouth full of cake.

"Well, it sounds like a dangerous place to play.

How about you girls staying a little closer to the church?"

Heather shrugged her shoulders. "It's not dangerous. It's pretty." She gave her father one of her rare smiles. "You know how Molly is. She thinks everything is dangerous."

Dave laughed and Mom smiled. "She has a point there," he said to Mom.

"Well, it looks like it's going to fall down," I said, "and the pond is deep."

"So?" Heather stared at me. "I know how to swim. Nothing's going to happen to me there."

"Maybe we'll all take a walk and see it one day," Mom said, smiling at Heather and me. "In the meantime, though, why don't you play here?"

Heather hid her face behind her glass of milk, and I noticed a little bulge under her tee shirt. "How about the locket?" I asked her. "Did you tell your father about that?"

"What locket, honey?" Dave leaned across the table toward her, but Heather shrank away from him, her hand covering the bump the locket made under her shirt.

"It's just this old thing." She pulled the chain out of her shirt and held up a tarnished heart. "I found it in the weeds by the pond."

Michael looked at me, his eyebrows raised. I knew what he was thinking — poor old Molly, taken in again.

"Well, isn't that nice?" Dave smiled at Heather. "I bet Jean could polish it up so it would look like new."

Mom reached for the locket, but Heather dropped it back down inside her shirt. "I like it just the way it is," she said.

"Does it open?" Mom asked. "People used to keep pictures or locks of hair in those."

Heather shook her head. "It's bent, so it won't open anymore."

"Can I have another piece of cake?" Michael asked, and dinner went on, without any more comments about the house or the locket.

When I woke up the next morning, the first thing I saw were gray clouds and dripping leaves. It had rained hard during the night, and it looked like more showers were on the way. As I pulled on my jeans and a long-sleeved shirt, I told myself that I wouldn't have to take Michael to the house after all. Even he wouldn't want to go walking through wet grass and muddy fields.

But I was wrong. He was waiting for me at the kitchen table, the remains of his breakfast in front of him, his windbreaker on the back of the chair. "I thought you were going to sleep all day," he said accusingly.

"It's going to rain, Michael. You don't still want to go, do you?"

"The weather forecast says there's only a thirty percent chance of showers," he said. "You aren't scared of getting wet, too?"

I scowled at him as I poured milk on my cereal. "Where's Heather?"

"Beats me." He grinned at me. "Maybe she's gone on ahead to tell Helen we're coming."

"Very funny." I ate my cereal in silence while he read the comics. After washing the dishes, I pulled on my windbreaker and followed him outside. "We take the path down to the cow pasture, cross the creek, and go through the woods," I told him.

In silence, we waded through the water, higher now because of the rain. The cows watched us mournfully from the other side of the fence. One of them made a little snorting sound and ran clumsily up the hill away from us, and the others followed more slowly, mooing in chorus.

"They sound like they're auditioning for parts in some Great Dairyland TV Special," Michael said, as we entered the woods, still wet and smelling of rain.

Although I didn't say it, I was sorry to leave the cows behind. The woods seemed unfriendly this morning; lost in gloom, they brooded like giants on the verge of waking from bad dreams. The only sounds were the cawing of crows somewhere ahead of us, the gurgle of the creek behind us, and the swishing noise our feet made brushing against the damp weeds bordering the path.

When we reached the edge of the woods, we paused and I pointed toward the house. Against sky of ragged clouds, the ruins looked grim and desolate. Behind the house, the trees swayed in the wind, and at its feet the pond lay, its water dark gray, its surface wrinkled.

"Well, Molly," Michael said solemnly, "I don't see any face at the window. I guess Helen isn't home today. She must be staying underground where it's all dry and snug." He laughed, and I punched his arm.

"Shut up," I hissed at him. To me, the windows were full of hidden eyes watching us. The murmuring of the wind in the woods, the sighing sound it made in the weeds, seemed to speak to me, warning me to leave. I shivered. "Come on, Michael, let's go back. It's going to rain any minute." I edged away from him, back toward the path and the haven of the woods.

But Michael ignored me. Without waiting to see if I would follow, he began climbing the hill toward the house.

"You'd better not go inside!" I called after him.

Glancing back at me over his shoulder, he said,

"Why not? Nobody's here. I don't even see a No Trespassing sign."

A gust of wind lifted the trailing vines on the house and sent them billowing toward us like outstretched arms. "Michael, come back!" I shouted, as the first drops of rain came pelting down out of the sky.

"There's still some roof on this side," he yelled. "Come on, Molly, we can stay dry."

As he disappeared through one of the windows, I ran after him, too scared to go home by myself. "Where are you?" I asked as I neared the house.

"Here." His face appeared in a window almost covered with honeysuckle. "You'll be dry in here."

My legs were shaking so hard, I could hardly manage to climb into the house. It was dark and cold; the floor beneath our feet creaked, and everything smelled of mold and decay and smoke. Huddling close to Michael, I glanced around fearfully, expecting to see something hideous in every shadow. But all I saw were spiderwebs and heaps of rusty beer cans and bottles, charred wood from bonfires, graffiti on the walls, discarded newspapers, and other assorted trash.

"See?" Michael said. "There's nothing here to be scared of. Looks like teenagers from Holwell come out here, and maybe bums. But no ghosts, Molly."

My teeth were chattering, but I nodded, pretending to believe him.

"This must have been a terrific house," Michael went on. "I bet the walls are more than two feet thick, all solid rock. The house was two or three stories high with a fireplace in every room. See?"

I looked up. We were standing in front of one fireplace and above our heads, jutting out of the wall, was another fireplace. Above that was what was left of the roof. Through the holes, rain fell, and I could see patches of gray sky.

"As soon as it stops raining, I'm going home," I told Michael. "You can stay here as long as you like."

Michael shrugged and began exploring the room. "I guess it burned down," he said, poking at a charred timber lying on the floor. "It must have been an incredible fire. Probably lit up the whole sky."

Without answering him, I went back to the window and looked out, hoping the rain had stopped. Down below me, I saw the pond. And something else.

"Michael!" I called to him, "Come here!"

"Why?" He had gone into the next room.

"It's Heather! She's down there by the pond!"

Michael joined me by the window, and we both stared at her, too surprised to move. She was standing by the water, her back to us, her hair swirling in the wind, absolutely soaked.

"What's she doing?" I whispered.

"I don't know, but she'll catch pneumonia if she stays there much longer." Michael pushed me aside and climbed out the window. "Heather," he yelled. "Get away from that water!"

She turned toward him, her mouth open in surprise, one hand clasping the locket. "Go away!" she shouted as he ran toward her.

I watched him grab her and try to drag her toward the house. She was doing her best to get away from him, twisting and turning, crying and screaming, begging him to leave her alone.

"Molly, help me!" Michael yelled, and I scrambled through the window, slipping and sliding as I ran down the hillside. Grabbing hold of Heather, I helped Michael drag her up the hill and into the house.

"What are you doing here?" she cried, still struggling to escape.

"Looking for you!" I shouted. "You know you aren't supposed to be here! Mom and Dave told you last night to stay closer to the church!"

"I'll go where I want to go!" Heather slumped suddenly, her eyes filled with tears, and she began to cry. "You're hurting my arms," she sobbed. "Let me go."

"Do you promise not to run away from us?" Michael scowled at her.

"Yes," Heather mumbled. "She's gone now anyway."

We let go of her, and she slumped on the floor between us, weeping, her face hidden in her hands. "You always make her go away," she wept, "but you'll be sorry. You'll be so sorry."

"See what I mean?" I turned to Michael. Surely he would believe me now.

"There's nobody here and there never was," Michael said scornfully. "You might be able to fool Molly with ghost stories, but you can't fool me. I know a lie when I hear one."

"Just wait till she comes!" Heather turned a look of pure hatred on Michael. "She'll get you first!"

But Michael just laughed. "What's taking her so long! Why can't she get me right now?"

"The time's not right," Heather said, gazing past us both. She stared out the window at the wind-lashed vines and dark clouds.

Michael laughed again. "Oh, I'm so scared," he said in a fake quaver.

"You should be." Heather stood up then and backed away from us, just as a stone tumbled from the wall above us and crashed at Michael's feet.

"There!" Heather shrieked as Michael and I stared at the stone. "She doesn't want you here. She wants me, just me!"

"Come on, Michael!" I tugged at his arm, trying to get him to leave the house. "Let's get out of here! I told you it wasn't safe."

"It was just the wind, that's all." Michael frowned at Heather. "But Molly's right. We shouldn't stay here in a storm. We're going home, and you're coming with us."

He grabbed one arm and I grabbed the other, and between the two of us we managed to drag Heather out of the house, down the hill, and into the woods. By the time we got to the creek, she was walking sullenly, like a prisoner on her way to a beheading.

When we had almost reached the church, Michael seized the chain around Heather's neck and looked at the locket before she could snatch it back.

"Those are your initials," he said. "You didn't find this anywhere. You had it all along, didn't you?"

"H.E.H," Heather said, a little smile passing over her face. "My initials, but not my name. You want to know whose name they stand for?"

Michael sighed, but I said, "Tell us, Heather. I want to know."

"Helen Elizabeth Harper," she whispered. "My friend and your enemy." Breaking away from us, she ran toward the church, leaving us to follow, soaked to the skin and, in my case at least, too scared to chase after her.

8

"HOW DO YOU explain it, Michael?" I asked him later. We were sitting at the kitchen table, drinking mugs of hot chocolate, still trying to get warm. Although I'd made a cup for Heather, she'd taken hers out to the carriage house.

"It's just a fantasy, Molly. Lots of kids have imaginary friends. Don't you remember Mr. Maypo?"

"How could I forget? Every time you did something bad, you blamed it on Mr. Maypo. Mom and I were both glad when he left for Timbuctoo." I took another sip of hot chocolate. "But this is different, Michael. You were only three when you had Mr. Maypo. Heather's seven. It's just not normal."

"Well, she's not normal. You know that, and

I know that, but Mom and Dave just won't admit it." Michael looked into his mug. "Ugh. Skin. I hate it when my hot chocolate gets skin on it!"

While he skimmed the surface of his hot chocolate with a spoon, I sipped mine thoughtfully. "But Michael," I said slowly, "suppose she's not making it up. Suppose Helen is real."

"Oh, Molly, honestly." Michael looked disgusted. "Ghosts do not exist. The kid is lying, and you're encouraging her. Can't you see? She's littler than we are, and she wants to make us think she's got some supernatural friend who'll beat us up or something if we're mean to her. It's so obvious; any idiot should be able to figure it out."

"Thanks a lot!" I felt my face turn red. "I'm not an idiot. If anybody is, you are!" I jumped up and went to the sink to rinse my cup.

"Hey, I'm sorry," Michael mumbled. "I'm just tired of hearing all this ghost talk."

"Maybe I have some kind of sixth sense that you don't have," I said. "Did you ever think of that?" I frowned at him, not ready to forgive him for calling me an idiot.

He shrugged. "Suppose we ride our bikes into Holwell and go to the library? I bet they have a book or something that would tell us all about that old house. Once you see that nobody named

Helen Elizabeth Harper ever lived there, maybe you'll realize what a liar Heather is."

"Do you want to go right now?" I squinted at the sky, trying to decide if it was going to rain any more today.

"Sure. I think we've had our thirty percent shower, don't you?"

We got our bikes out from under the porch and rode down Clark Road toward town. It was a long way, and I was glad the rain had cooled things off. On a hot day, I would never have made it up some of the hills between our house and Holwell.

We found the library on a quiet street near the park and locked our bikes. Inside it was small and friendly, more like a living room in somebody's house than a library. Except for all the books, of course. There were hundreds of them, jammed into shelves lining the walls and forming alcoves near the windows.

"Can I help you find something?" a woman asked as I began riffling through the card catalogue.

"I hope so." Michael smiled up at her. "My sister and I just moved into an old church out on Clark Road and when we were out in the woods today, we found the ruins of an old house. It looked like it burned down a long time ago.

We just wondered if you had any information about it."

"Oh, yes." The librarian smiled. "I know what house you mean."

She led us to a row of file cabinets at the back of the room. "We have several files on historical homes in and around Holwell," she said, flicking through the folders in one of the drawers. "Is this the house?"

She laid a newspaper clipping down on the table where we could see it. "It burned down about a hundred years ago. A terrible fire," she murmured, pointing to a blurred photograph of the house by the pond.

"One of our local historians wrote this article several years ago." Setting the clipping aside before I had a chance to read it, she produced an old photograph. "Here is the house before it burned," she said. "Lovely isn't it?"

I nodded. In the picture I saw a big stone house, standing on a hill with a lawn sweeping down to a pond. On the terrace sat three people: a man, a woman, and a girl. The man and woman sat close together, their hands clasped, but the girl sat apart, her face turned away. I stared at it, wishing the people were bigger and easier to see.

"That's Mr. and Mrs. Miller," the librarian said, pointing to the man and woman.

Michael nudged me, and I smiled, relieved that

their name was Miller, not Harper. But the librarian wasn't quite finished. "And this," she went on, her finger lingering on the girl, "is Mrs. Miller's daughter, Helen."

"Helen?" I stared into the woman's face, my heart thumping.

She nodded and turned the picture over. Someone had written in a spidery, old-fashioned hand, "Mabel, Robert, and Mabel's girl, Helen. Taken in June, 1886, at Harper House."

"Harper House?" It was Michael's turn to ask questions now. I was sure I couldn't have said a word if my life depended on it. "Are you certain that's what it's called?"

"Why, of course. It's written right here." The librarian looked at the writing again, as if she were double-checking. "You see, the house was built a few generations earlier by Harold Harper. It stayed in the family till Mabel's first husband, Joseph Harper — that would be Helen's father — died. When Mabel remarried, her name changed to Miller, but folks kept on calling it Harper House. Unfortunately, Mr. and Mrs. Miller didn't live there long before it burned down."

"Were they caught in the fire?" Michael leaned across the table toward the librarian, his eyes big behind his glasses. In the silence following his question, I could hear a fly buzzing against the window behind me.

"Yes, the whole family was killed." The librarian pushed the old newspaper clipping across the table toward us. "You can read Miss Hawkins' article. It's a very complete account, right down to the ghost stories people tell about the house."

I backed away from the clipping, thinking that I had heard all I wanted to, but Michael bent over it eagerly. "Listen to this, Molly," he said, his voice rising in excitement. "Mr. and Mrs. Miller's bodies were never found. They must be buried somewhere under the wreckage. No wonder people think the place is haunted!"

I stared at him, feeling the hairs on the back of my neck quiver. "What about Helen?" I whispered. "What happened to her?"

"Oh," the librarian said, answering for Michael. "She apparently escaped from the house and ran into the pond. It was dark, and I suppose she was confused or frightened. At any rate, she drowned. According to the newspaper account, her body was buried in Saint Swithin's graveyard."

"Where's that?" Michael asked.

"Why, it's just where you live." The librarian smiled at him. "Surely you've noticed the little burial ground behind the church."

As Michael nodded and told her about the

tombstone under the oak tree, I watched the fly struggle to find a way out of the library. I wanted to find an escape too, but every word I'd heard confirmed my fear that Heather had somehow allied herself with a ghost. What I wasn't sure of was the danger — was Helen as wicked as Heather made her out to be, or was she merely a lost child looking for someone to love her?

Edging a little closer to the librarian, I said, "What kind of ghost stories do people tell about Harper House?"

"It's all in the clipping," she said a bit impatiently, flicking her fingernail at the article which Michael was still reading. "But, if I remember correctly, people claim the child's ghost haunts the graveyard and the pond."

A frown crossed her face. "They actually believe the poor girl is responsible for some of the drownings in the pond, but you know how people are. They're always looking for some sort of supernatural cause for the simplest things."

"People have drowned in the pond?" I thought of Heather standing at the water's edge in the pouring rain.

The librarian nodded. "It's a pretty place, and it's tempting on a hot day. Children don't need ghosts to lure them into a nice, cool pond." She smiled at me and added, "A child drowned last summer in the municipal pool, but nobody blamed *that* on a ghost."

"In other words," Michael said, "you don't believe the stories." From his tone of voice, I could tell he was looking for an ally.

She smiled and shook her head. "I've picnicked by Harper Pond many times, and I never saw a thing but birds and butterflies." As she began gathering up the papers on the table, she paused and gazed at the picture of the Millers and Helen sitting on the porch, innocent of the terrible event that would soon destroy them. "Nevertheless, it was certainly a tragedy, wasn't it?"

As soon as Michael and I were outside, I turned to him. "Well, what do you have to say now?"

He shoved his glasses into place on his nose and frowned. "Heather must have talked to somebody, Molly. The last time Mr. Simmons came to mow the graveyard — he must have told her about Harper House."

"But, Michael, he didn't even know Helen's grave was there. He couldn't have told her what those initials stood for."

Michael shook his head and began to pedal his bike down the street toward home. "She's made it all up somehow," he yelled back at me. "I know it's not a ghost, Molly. It's just not possible."

"Wait for me, Michael," I shouted, pumping hard. "Don't go so fast!"

He slowed down and let me catch up, but I could tell he didn't want to talk about Harper House or Helen. The little wheels in his brain were spinning round and round, trying frantically to come up with a rational solution. I had a feeling that he was just as scared as I was, maybe even more scared because science didn't have an explanation for something like Helen.

All of a sudden, Michael slowed to a stop beside a road sign almost hidden by the honeysuckle climbing over it. "Look, Molly, this is Harper House Road." He pointed at a narrow dirt road curving up out of sight over a hill. "Let's see where it goes."

Before I could tell him that I'd had enough of Harper House for one day, if not for the rest of my life, he took off in a cloud of dust. Not wanting to ride home alone, I followed him, hoping the hill wouldn't be too steep for me. By the time I had huffed and puffed my way to the top, Michael was vanishing around a sharp curve at the bottom. Putting on my brakes, I flew after him, my hair blowing straight back from my face, sure I was going to shoot over my handlebars and split my head open. By a miracle, I managed to skid safely to a stop on a narrow stone bridge just behind Michael.

Mr. Simmons was so startled by our sudden appearance that he almost dropped his fishing pole. "Well, well," he said, "where did you two come from? Straight down out of the sky?"

"That house," Michael said, pointing to the ruins just visible through the trees. "Did you tell Heather about it?"

"Heather?" Mr. Simmons fiddled with his pipe for a moment, then puffed a fragrant cloud of smoke into the air. "You mean your little sister, the one who found the gravestone?"

Michael and I nodded, but Mr. Simmons shook his head. "I haven't seen her since then. And why would I tell her about Harper House? It ought to be torn down, if you ask me. It's a haven for all sorts of goings-on — a disgrace to the town of Holwell. No place for a child to play, that's for sure."

I looked at Michael, but his eyes shifted away from mine. From the frown on his face, I knew he was struggling to invent a new theory to explain Heather's knowing so much about Helen. Turning to Mr. Simmons, I asked him if he knew Harper House was haunted.

"Who told you that?" he asked.

"The lady at the library," Michael answered.

"She showed us some old newspaper articles." Using his scornful scientist voice, he told Mr. Simmons what the librarian had said.

"Miss Williams told you all that?" Mr. Simmons laughed and shook his head. "She ought to have more sense. A grown woman scaring kids with ghost stories."

Michael frowned at Mr. Simmons. "She didn't scare me! I don't believe in that kind of stuff." Jerking his head toward me, he added, "*She's* the one who's scared to death of Helen. I don't know which one's worse, her or Heather."

"You're just fooling yourself, Michael!" Gripping the handlebars of my bike, I leaned toward him, angry that he'd made me look foolish in front of Mr. Simmons. "Helen is every bit as real as you are, and you know it!"

Mr. Simmons looked from me to Michael and then back at me. Pausing to fiddle with his pipe, he said, "Ghost or no ghost, you kids stay away from Harper House. The walls are about to cave in, and at least three children have drowned in the pond. The water's not fit for swimming; it's murky and full of weeds."

"The librarian told us that some people think Helen's ghost lures children into the pond." I gazed past Mr. Simmons at the water's surface shimmering through the leaves. It looked very peaceful in the afternoon sunlight.

"Well, now, I don't know about that," Mr. Simmons said, "but I do know a girl drowned three years ago. She was one of these lonely little creatures. No friends, nobody who seemed to care much about her — you know the kind. Well, she disappeared one day, and this is where they finally found her." He gestured through the trees at the glittering water.

"Ten feet under," he added, "and all tangled up in weeds. I hope I never see anything that sad again."

I looked at Michael and shivered, but he was staring at the ground, his forehead wrinkled.

"Well, now, I didn't mean to upset you," Mr. Simmons said a little too loudly. "I just thought you should know the pond's no place to play." Pulling a watch out of his pocket, he mumbled, "My goodness, it's after five already. Time I got myself home."

He tossed his rod and reel into the back of his pickup truck and turned to Michael. "Do you like to fish, boy?"

Michael shrugged. "I don't know how."

"Well, I'll tell you what. Next time I come over to mow the graveyard, I'll bring along an extra rod and teach you how. Would you like that?"

Michael grinned and said he'd love it. Mr.

Simmons got into his truck, threw it into gear, and bounced away in a cloud of dust.

"See? He doesn't believe in those old stories either," Michael said.

Without answering, I got on my bike and started pedaling slowly back up the hill. No matter what Michael or Mr. Simmons thought, I believed in Helen, and I was afraid she had some sort of hold on Heather. They were linked, I thought, in so many ways: by their initials, by their loneliness, by their mothers' deaths.

Like the girl Mr. Simmons had just told us about, Heather was one of those lonely little creatures, friendless and unhappy, and I was frightened. Not for myself — but for Heather.

9

AS MICHAEL AND I rode our bikes down the driveway, we saw Mom standing on the back porch, her hands on her hips. "Where have you been?" she said as we braked to a stop.

"At the library," I said, wheeling my bike to its place under the porch.

"And then we saw Mr. Simmons." Michael was too excited to notice that Mom was not smiling. "Guess what? He's going to take me fishing the next time he comes to cut the grass."

"But you were supposed to be here watching Heather." Mom folded her arms tightly across her chest and frowned at me. "Didn't we talk about that just the other day?"

"She was out in the carriage house with Dave when we left," I said. "You were painting, and I know you don't like being disturbed, so Michael and I just decided to go. I thought it would be all right."

As Michael started to say something in my defense, he was interrupted by Dave. He stepped out on the porch to join Mom, and Heather was right behind him, peering around his legs, her pale eyes on Michael and me.

"Do you two have any idea what a scare you gave us?" Dave asked, his voice rising. "We couldn't find any of you! We called and called. Finally I found Heather way down on the other side of the creek near that ruin you told your mother about. She said you took her there and then ran off and left her."

I stared at him. "We didn't take her anywhere!"

But he went right on talking. "Why do you treat her so badly? You've made her life miserable ever since we moved out here." He was yelling now, and his face was red. "Heather's just a little girl, a very sensitive little girl! Why can't you treat her decently? What's wrong with you two?"

As Dave continued to accuse us of tormenting Heather, the poor little victim peeked at us, smiling slyly. She was enjoying every minute of his tirade.

"Dave, please." Mom laid her hand on his arm, trying to calm him down. "Don't talk to Molly and Michael that way. There must be some mis-understanding."

Dave turned from us to Mom. "That's right, Jean! Take their side as usual!" Brushing Mom's hand away, he led Heather down the steps, past Michael and me, and strode across the driveway toward the van.

"Where are you going?" Mom called after him, her voice quavering. "Dinner's ready, Dave." She started to follow him, but stopped, halfway down the steps.

"You all eat it. I'm taking my daughter out for dinner. She needs to get away for a while." Without looking at us, Dave slammed the van door and gunned the motor. As he roared down the driveway, I saw Heather smile at us.

"I hate him!" I looked at Mom, but she had already turned away from me. I followed her up the steps. "We didn't take Heather into the woods, Mom. She lied!"

Mom paused at the doorway and wiped her eyes with the back of her hand. "But you could have stayed here or taken her to the library with you," she said. "None of this would have hap-pened if you had done what I asked you to."

Michael grabbed my arm and stopped me from following Mom into the kitchen. "Drop it," he whispered. "She's really upset, and you'll just make things worse." His face wore its worried expression, making him look more like a little old man than usual.

Pulling away from him, I crossed the kitchen to the stove. Mom was stirring the stew she'd cooked. "I'm sorry," I said softly.

"It's all right." She watched the stew bubble and poked it with the spoon.

"Are we going to eat?" Michael asked.

"Go ahead, help yourselves." Mom handed me the spoon.

"How about you?" I asked as she walked to the door.

"I'm not hungry." Pushing the door open, she stepped outside.

"Where are you going?" Michael ran out on the porch behind her.

"For a walk." Her voice was sharp. "You eat your dinner. I'll be back soon."

Silently I filled two plates with stew, while Michael poured our milk. After we'd eaten a few mouthfuls, Michael said, "She was crying."

"I know." We looked at each other. "It's all Heather's fault. Did you see the way she was grinning when Dave was yelling at us?"

Michael nodded. "It's just what she wants — to cause enough trouble to ruin things for Mom and Dave."

"Why can't Dave see what she's doing? He's blind to everything she does." I pushed my plate away, half my stew uneaten. The kitchen was getting dark, and I felt sad looking at the three empty plates stacked on the counter. "Do you think we should go find Mom?"

Michael polished off the last of his stew by wiping his plate with a piece of bread. Then he gulped down his milk and brushed away the white mustache it left on his upper lip. "I guess so."

Turning on the kitchen light to make the room look cheerier, I hesitated in the doorway. The sky was gray and the trees were dark shapes, glittering with lightning bugs. A breeze shushed through the grass, rustling the leaves and bringing with it the scent of honeysuckle. The night seemed very still and private, and I wasn't sure I really wanted to leave the safety of the kitchen.

"Molly, are you going to stand there all night?" Michael stared at me from the driveway; the kitchen light shone on his glasses, giving him an owlish look.

"I'm coming." Folding my arms across my chest, I followed him across the yard. The grass was cold and wet, and I could feel it soaking through my running shoes. Glancing back at the lit windows, I felt homesick for Baltimore.

"Michael," I said, getting him to stop for a minute. "It was never this bad before we came here. Heather was pretty awful, but not like she is now. And we got along with Dave all right. He and Mom never had fights then."

"I know. I was thinking that too."

"It's living out here." I looked past him, at the oak tree's dark, shaggy shape dominating the sky, towering over everything else. It was Helen's influence, I thought. Whether Heather had dreamed her up or not, she had made things worse. Day by day, our lives seemed to grow unhappier, as if she had the ability somehow to reach out from the grave and touch us all with her misery.

"Maybe we should do what Mom said." I turned to Michael, studying his face in the moonlight. "Maybe we should really try to be nice to Heather."

"Are you kidding?"

"I'm worried about her, Michael. You heard what Dave said. She went back to the pond, back to Harper House. I know you don't believe she really sees a ghost, but that's not the point. Whatever makes her go there is dangerous." I paused, knowing Michael thought I was foolish. "Even Mr. Simmons thinks it's a bad place to play. He doesn't believe in ghosts — he just knows kids have drowned there."

Michael sighed. "Okay, Molly. *You* play with her; *you* try to be nice to her. See how far it gets you." Shrugging my hand from his arm, he started walking toward the graveyard. "I'm not having anything to do with that kid," he called back to me.

"Michael, is that you?" Mom came toward us.

"We were worried about you," Michael said. "It's dark."

She put her arms out and drew the two of us close to her. Then we walked back to the church, Mom in the middle, Michael and I holding her hands.

"I'm sorry I got so upset," she said, pausing at the bottom of the porch steps. The kitchen light slanted out the door, and shone on her face and hair, hiding her eyes in shadow. "I'm so worried about us, Heather, everything."

"I'm sorry too, Mom. Michael and I just can't get along with her. Or Dave. We do try, honest we do."

"I know, Molly." Mom gave me a hug. "She's such an unhappy little girl. I feel so sorry for her, but I don't know how to reach her, how to make her happy. Sometimes I think it might have been better for all of us if she had continued living with her grandmother."

She sat down on the steps, hugging her knees against her chest as if she were cold. "I tried to talk to Dave about her before you all came home, but he said I wasn't trying. He said I didn't love her enough." Mom looked at us, her eyes filling with tears again. "She isn't easy to love," she said sadly.

"Here they come," Michael said as the van's headlights swept across us.

We watched Heather and Dave get out of the van. Heather was eating an ice cream cone as she walked toward us, licking it very slowly to make it last as long as possible. Without saying a word, she climbed the steps, giving us a wide berth. I tried to force myself to reach out, to speak to her, but I couldn't. Silently I watched her vanish into the kitchen as Dave lumbered up the steps behind her.

"I'll put her to bed," he said, without stopping to look at us.

Mom stood up and followed him into the house, leaving Michael and me on the steps. For a while, neither of us said a word. We just sat there, listening to the crickets chirping under the porch.

"Well," Michael said finally, "we might as well go to bed. The little monster is probably asleep now."

"Until she wakes us all up with another nightmare." Shivering in the cool night air, I stood up and started to follow Michael into the house. A rustling in the leaves made me glance over my shoulder. "Michael!" I grasped his arm and pulled him back. "Look!" I pointed toward the graveyard.

"What?" He stared past my pointing finger.

"Didn't you see it?" I clung to him, trembling. "There was a light. It's gone now, but I saw it. Down at the end, under the oak tree. A sort of glimmer."

Michael shook his head. "It must have been a lightning bug. Honestly, Molly, there isn't a ghost lurking among the tombstones."

"I *saw* it. A bluish glow. It wasn't a lightning bug!"

"Let's go in." Prying my fingers from his arm, Michael opened the screen door, and I hurried after him into the brightly lit kitchen, shutting not only the screen door but the wooden door as well.

"You still haven't come up with an explanation for Heather's knowing so much about Harper House," I reminded him.

He frowned and looked around the kitchen as if he expected to see an explanation written on the walls. "It could be ESP," he said thoughtfully. "I didn't use to believe in all that paranormal stuff, but there is scientific evidence that a few people have some sort of extrasensory perception. I suppose it could explain Heather's knowing so much about Helen."

"You mean she has some sixth sense?"

He nodded. "It's better than believing she communicates with a ghost."

I shook my head. "You haven't seen as much as I have."

"Oh, Molly." Michael started walking down the hall toward his room. "Give it up, will you?"

He went into his room and closed the door, and I tiptoed into my room. Heather seemed to be asleep, so I got into bed as quietly as I could and pulled my Walkman out from under my pillow. Before I had a chance to turn it on, I heard Mom's voice through the bedroom wall.

"I don't see how you can continue to take her word against theirs," she was saying. "You know perfectly well she makes up all sorts of things just to cause trouble!"

"That's not true, Jean." Dave's voice rose. "Can't you see what they're trying to do?"

"No, I can't. I know my own children, and they have no reason to make you and me unhappy. They were delighted when we got married. It's Heather who wants to come between us, not Molly and Michael!" Mom's voice rose too.

As the argument grew louder, I wanted to bury my head under my pillow, but a movement from Heather's bed drew my attention to her. She was sitting up, listening to every word and smiling.

"You!" I yelled at her. "This is all your doing, isn't it? You love every quarrel they have!"

"Your mother is a witch," Heather said, "and she makes my daddy unhappy. I wish she were dead, and you and Michael, too!"

"My mother has done everything she can to make you happy," I shouted, "and all you do is throw it back in her face. You're a little monster!"

"My daddy doesn't think so. He loves me. He loves me more than he loves her, and if I want him to, he'll take me away from here and all of you." She glared across the room at me, her face fierce in the moonlight.

"You're a liar!"

"You better watch what you say to me!" Heather was sitting straight up, her hair falling in tangled curls across her forehead. "I can make you sorry, Molly. You and Michael and your mother!"

The door opened and Michael entered the room. "What's going on in here?"

Heather leapt to her feet, standing in the middle of the bed, her fists clenched. "Wait till Helen comes!" she screamed.

Dave rushed into the room just then, and Heather collapsed in a heap on her bed, weeping hysterically. Dave rushed to her side and lifted her into his arms. "What is it, Heather? What's wrong?"

"Daddy, Daddy," she wept, clinging to him.

"What have you done to her now?" Dave turned on Michael and me as Mom appeared behind him, her face pale, her hair flying.

"Nothing!" Michael shouted.

"She was listening to you all fighting," I told Mom, "and gloating! You should have heard her."

"Daddy, Daddy," Heather sobbed. "Make them leave me alone."

"There, there, Heather. Daddy's here. It's all right." He rocked her back and forth in his arms, soothing her as if she were a baby.

"Michael," Mom said softly, "go back to your room. We'll talk about this in the morning."

Michael started to object, saw the expression on Mom's face, and sidled past Dave and Heather. "We didn't do anything," he whispered to Mom.

She nodded and gave him a hug. "Just try to get some sleep, honey."

As soon as he was gone, Mom turned to me. "I'm sorry you heard us quarreling," she said. "I'll tuck you in."

When Mom bent over me, I reached up to hug her. "She hates us," I whispered. "All of us. She scares me, Mom." Tears welled up in my eyes, and Mom sat down beside me.

"Don't let her upset you, Molly," she whispered back. "She's a very disturbed little girl. I know it's hard for you. It's hard for me too, but try to understand that she's just as unhappy as you are, probably more so."

"Come on, Jean," Dave said softly. "Heather's asleep now."

Before he left the room, though, Dave turned back and looked at me. "I don't want any more of this, Molly. I mean it." Then he was gone.

Before closing my eyes, I looked at Heather. Her back was turned toward me, and I could hear the sound of deep, regular breathing. It was hard for me to believe that she could drop off to sleep so quickly after causing so much trouble, but for the five minutes that I watched her, I saw no sign that she was faking. Satisfied that she was truly asleep, I rolled away from her, closed my eyes, and tried to let my Walkman relax me.

Just as I was hovering on the edge of a nice dream about our old neighborhood, I heard Heather's bed creak and the unmistakable sound of a bare foot on the floor. Without opening my eyes, I sensed her standing by me, watching me. Then she went to the window and shoved the screen up.

I lay still, afraid that she would hear the sound of my heart beating in the silence. But after a few seconds, she climbed quietly out the window and dropped to the ground below.

I waited a couple of minutes, then got up and

peered out the window. In the moonlight, I saw her making her way across the lawn toward the graveyard. At the far end, through the hedge, a bluish glow illuminated the leaves of the oak tree. As I watched, Heather disappeared through the gate.

Shivering with fear, I climbed out the window and ran through the grass, already cold and wet with dew. Keeping in the shadow of the hedge, I crept past the gate, staying outside the graveyard, until I reached the black shade of the oak tree. Dropping to my knees, I peered through the hedge at Helen's grave.

Dimly lit by the blue glow I'd seen from the house, Heather held out a jar of wild flowers as if she were making an offering. The silver locket gleamed on her chest, and her eyes glittered.

"Helen," she whispered, "Helen. Are you here?"

Too frightened to breathe, I saw the glimmer of blue light shape itself into the figure of a girl no bigger than Heather. She wore a white dress, and her hair, as dark as Heather's, tumbled in waves down her back. Her features were indistinct, her eyes in shadow, but I knew who she was.

"I'm here," the girl said. Her voice was low and cold.

Heather smiled. "How beautiful you are," she

whispered as Helen took the flowers and bent her face to smell their fragrance.

They regarded each other silently for a few moments. Then Heather spoke once more. "They have been cruel to me again," she said. "I've told them you're coming, but I don't think they believe me. Do something soon, Helen. Make them sorry." Heather leaned toward the dim figure, imploring her.

"Soon." Helen's voice was like the winter wind blowing through a field of weeds, dry and cruel. "Very soon."

"And then we'll be together all the time? You'll never leave me? You'll always love me?" Heather gazed at Helen, desperation in her voice and gestures.

"For all eternity," Helen sighed. "You and I, Heather. We'll never be alone again. I promise you." One pale hand, almost transparent, glimmered near the locket, making it shine with borrowed radiance.

"How about Daddy? He'll be with us, won't he?" Heather took a tiny step backward, away from the hand touching the locket.

Helen didn't answer. Her image wavered like a reflection on the water when a breeze ruffles the surface. Then she was gone, and the graveyard seemed to plunge into darkness. Heather cried out, reaching toward the air where Helen's shape had vanished.

"Helen, Helen, don't leave me!" she cried and fell to her knees, knocking over the jar of wild flowers in front of the tombstone. As she began to gather them up, sobbing for Helen to return, I backed away from the hedge toward the safety of the house.

Running across the grass in the moonlight, I was afraid to look back for fear of seeing Helen in pursuit. As soon as I reached the window, I scrambled through, heedless of the noise I was making, and flung myself into bed.

I don't know how long I lay there, shivering with fright, waiting for Heather to come back. When I heard her at the window, I shut my eyes tight, praying that she was alone.

"Just wait, Molly," Heather whispered in my ear in a voice almost as chilling as Helen's. "Just wait till Helen comes. You'll be sorry then for all the things you've done to me."

10

IF I SLEPT any more that night, I don't remember it. As soon as the gray light of dawn glimmered at the window, I slipped out of bed and tiptoed down the hall to Michael's room.

"Go away," he mumbled when I shook his shoulder. "It's too early to get up."

"It's important, Michael!"

"Nothing's that important." He tried to pull the blankets over his head. "It's not even five-thirty, Molly. Are you crazy?"

"Michael, please get up. Please. I saw Helen, I *saw* her!" My voice quivered and my heart beat faster as I remembered what I'd seen in the graveyard. "She was horrible, more horrible even than I imagined."

Michael squinted at me. "Are you having a nightmare or something?"

"Will you listen to me, Michael?" I grabbed his shoulders and shook him again. "Heather climbed out the window last night, and I followed her to the graveyard. Helen was there — I saw her. And I heard her. She didn't have eyes, Michael, just dark holes, and her skin was bluish white like a dead person's. She said she was coming, she'd do what Heather wants; then she vanished." I clung to him, afraid that at any moment Helen would appear, seeking some sort of horrible vengeance. "What are we going to do?"

Michael stared at me. He was wide awake, but I could tell that he didn't believe me. "Come on, Molly," he said, pulling away from me to sit up. "You must have had a nightmare. Maybe because of that picture Mrs. Williams showed us. And then the fight with Dave, and Heather making that big scene. Nobody went to the graveyard last night. Not Heather, not you. You dreamed it." He spoke slowly and calmly as if he were trying to convince himself as well as me.

I looked away, fiddling with my hair, wishing it had been a dream. I shook my head. "No, Michael, I didn't dream it."

"You say Heather climbed out the window. How did she get back in?" He groped for his glasses and settled them on his nose.

"The same way." I stood up as he got out of

bed and pulled a sweatshirt on over his pajamas.

"I'll prove you dreamed it," he said confidently. "Come on."

Grabbing his bathrobe, I followed him down the hall and out the kitchen door. The morning mist swirled across the lawn like dry-ice fog in a Dracula movie, hiding the hedge as well as the graveyard. Somewhere a crow cawed, and I shivered as I felt the wet grass under my bare feet. "Where are we going?" I whispered, fearing he meant to lead me to Helen's grave.

Shushing me, Michael went toward my bedroom window. "She could have climbed out," he said, "but she's too short to get back in that way."

"How about this?" I pointed to an old wooden box lying on its side under the window. "She probably stood on it, and it fell over when she got inside."

Michael righted the box under the window. "I guess she *could* have," he said doubtfully.

"You're spying on me again!"

My scalp prickled at the sound of Heather's voice. She was standing inside, her face pressed against the window screen.

"You better leave me alone!" Heather's voice rose shrilly. "I know what you want to do — you want to make Helen go away, but she won't, not unless I tell her to. And I never will!"

I looked at Michael, but he was scowling at Heather. "You can't scare *me,*" he said scornfully.

"She's going to get you!" Heather's voice dropped to a hiss. "Just wait and see. It won't be long now."

"Heather?" Dave came into the room. "What's going on? Where's Molly?"

"Out there," Heather said. "Spying on me." Her voice quavered. "Her and Michael. They won't leave me alone." She was crying now, and I could hear Dave trying to comfort her.

Climbing up on the box, Michael peered into the room. "She's lying!"

Dave came to the window. "How long is this going to go on? Can't you see what you're doing to her? What kind of a little monster are you anyway?"

Michael glared at him. "Why don't you open your eyes and see what she's really like?" he yelled.

"Michael!" Mom took Dave's place at the window. "You and Molly get in here this minute!"

"We didn't do anything to her," Michael said without moving from the box.

"I said, come inside!" Mom frowned at us. "What are you doing out there in your pajamas at six o'clock in the morning? Wasn't last night enough? Do we have to start out today with the same business?"

Hearing the desperation in her voice, I plucked at Michael's sleeve. "Do what she says," I mumbled.

Shaking his head at the unfairness of it all, Michael jumped down from the box and the two of us walked slowly around the house to the back door. My pajamas were wet with dew from the knees down, and my feet were numb with cold. "Do you believe me now?" I asked Michael as we hesitated on the porch, afraid to go inside and face everybody's anger.

"Not about the ghost," Michael said without looking at me. "But I think she did go outside last night."

"And I followed her and I saw Helen." I tried to make him meet my eyes, but he edged away from me and opened the screen door.

"You imagined that part," he insisted. "You heard Heather giving her spiel, pretending to talk to Helen, and you thought you actually saw her. You didn't see Helen, though, Molly. You didn't! She doesn't exist!"

He walked ahead of me down the hall and went into his room, closing the door behind him. Taking the hint, I went reluctantly to my room. Dave and Heather were gone, but Mom was sitting on my bed waiting for me.

"Get dressed," she said, as if the very effort of speaking exhausted her. "You'll catch your death in those wet pajamas." She stood up wearily. "I want to talk to you and Michael later. I'll be in the kitchen."

What Mom had to say wasn't very different from what she'd said the night before. "I thought you were going to cooperate," she said finally. "I hoped you were going to try to be nicer, but what do I wake up to? Heather crying because you and Michael are spying on her. Dave upset and angry. And you two outside in your pajamas. I just don't see how you could do it, not after the talk we had before you went to bed!"

"You don't understand, Mom!" I threw myself at her, trying to climb into her lap. "There's something awful here, and it's making everything worse. It's not Michael and me. It's not even just Heather. It's something out there —" I gestured out the door toward the graveyard. "Under the oak tree, a grave."

"What are you talking about?" Mom grasped my shoulders and held me away from her, staring into my eyes.

"It's Helen," I screamed. "It's Helen!" Then I began crying too hard to talk.

"She thinks Heather has called up a ghost or something," I heard Michael tell Mom, using his mature, scientific voice. "Heather talks about a girl named Helen all the time, but Helen's just something she's dreamed up. You know, to scare us with — not me, actually. Just Molly."

"Oh, Molly, Molly." Mom rocked me, trying to make me stop crying. "Not that ghost business again. If I'd known having a graveyard on our property was going to upset you so much, I'd never have moved us out here."

"It's not my imagination," I gulped. "I saw Helen."

Mom sighed. "Dave says you have a terrible fear of death," she said, "and it's manifesting itself in your belief in ghosts."

"Why don't you ask Heather about it?" I pulled away from Mom, angry that she would turn to Dave for an explanation of my behavior and then actually believe him.

"Ask me what?" Heather and Dave appeared in the kitchen doorway.

"Tell them about Helen." I jumped off Mom's lap and confronted Heather angrily.

Shrinking back against Dave, the little girl looked up at me, her eyes wide and clear. "Who?"

"Helen, your great friend. Tell them what she's going to do when she comes!" I glared at her, furious. "Tell them how you meet her in the graveyard and in the ruins of the Harper House!"

"Daddy, Daddy, what's she talking about?"

Heather turned away from me and pressed her face against Dave's side, her arms encircling his waist. "Make her leave me alone. She's scaring me!"

"That's enough, Molly." Dave gave Heather a hug. "It's all right, honey." He and Mom looked at each other as if they were unsure what to make of me. "Are you ready to leave, Jean?" he asked.

"Leave?" I turned to Mom. "Where are you going?"

"Oh, we thought we'd take Heather with us when we go shopping. Dave needs to go to the clay supplier, and I'm low on some of my paints." Mom toyed with her coffee cup as if she were ashamed to meet Michael's and my stare. "We'll be back sometime this afternoon."

"But what about us?" I asked. "Why can't we go?"

"We thought it would be better to separate you two and Heather," Dave said. "You're old enough to take care of yourselves."

As I started to protest, Michael interrupted. "That sounds like a good idea. Come on, Molly." He picked up his empty cereal bowl and glass and carried them to the sink. "Have a nice time," he said to Mom. "With her."

He left the room without looking at anybody, obviously expecting me to follow him. I hesitated for a moment, thinking Mom might change her mind and stay home with us, but she stood up and slung her purse over her shoulder.

"You and Michael behave yourselves," she said. "We should be home around three." Giving me a quick hug and kiss, she whispered, "And please, Molly, no more talk about ghosts." She looked at me as if she were worried about my sanity. "I know you're a very imaginative girl, but don't get carried away."

I stood in the doorway watching them get into the van. As Dave pulled away, Heather peered out of the back window. When she saw me, she stuck out her tongue.

"Molly?" Michael came up behind me, carrying his collecting gear. "Want to go down to the swamp with me?"

Normally I would have said no, but I didn't want to stay in the house by myself. Not today. Not with Helen so close. So I helped him pack lunches, and we set off for the swamp, following the creek away from Harper House.

Although I couldn't help worrying about snakes, Michael assured me we were safe, and slowly I began to relax and enjoy myself. I actually helped him catch a couple of salamanders. He had brought along a plastic bowl which he lined with moss. Adding a little water and a rock, he put the salamanders into their new home and fed them a few insects.

"Are you hungry?" he asked me.

"Sure." We sat down on a fallen tree and ate our sandwiches. A bullfrog boomed every now and then from somewhere in the swamp, and I watched a snapping turtle hoist himself out of the water to bask in the sunlight. Overhead a bluejay screamed and a crow answered.

"Do you really think I imagined seeing Helen?" I asked Michael, unable even here to forget what had happened in the graveyard.

"You must have." Michael took a big bite of his sandwich and chewed it noisily.

"Then why do you think she seemed so real?" I watched the turtle flop back into the water. "She was just as real as you are."

"Maybe — and, believe me, I hate to say it — Dave is right about your being scared of dying."

"But aren't you scared? Isn't *everybody*?"

Michael poked a stick into the water and watched the long-legged skater bugs skitter away from it. "It's like nuclear war, Molly. If I think about it, I get really scared, so I don't let myself. There's no sense in worrying about things you can't change."

I envied the way my little brother could dismiss scary thoughts. "What do you think happens when people die, though? Do you think part of you lives forever?" I watched him stir the water with his stick, frowning down at our reflections. "Or do you think it's just like going to sleep and never waking up?" I persisted.

"I don't know." Michael turned to me. "I told you I don't like to think about things like that."

"Then you are scared. Just like me."

"Maybe. But I don't go around claiming I saw a ghost."

"No." I gazed out across the water. "But suppose you did see one, Michael. If Helen is real, it means something. Think what it would be like to be alone for all eternity." I shivered and drew my knees up to my chest. Hugging them, I realized how unhappy Helen must be. How afraid. How alone.

"If she's alone," I mused more to myself than to Michael, "she must want a friend, someone to keep her company. Those children, the ones Mr. Simmons told us about, suppose Helen lured them into the pond so they'd stay with her forever?"

Michael took off his glasses and rubbed them on his tee shirt. "You're really getting morbid, Molly."

"Suppose Helen wants Heather to be with her too?" I remembered the struggle she had put up when we dragged her away from the pond.

"Heather could be the one who's in danger, Michael, not us."

Michael sighed in exasperation. "If I hear much more about Helen, I'm going to get as crazy as you and Heather are!" Rising to his feet, he picked up the bowl of salamanders. "You're really a lot of fun," he added when I started to cry. I just couldn't help it.

"Where are you going?" I called as he walked off into the woods.

"Back to the church," he said without looking at me.

11

·❖·

AS SOON as I came out of the woods behind the church, I knew something was wrong. The air shimmered with heat, and it was very still. No breeze ruffled the leaves of the maples; no bird sang; no car sped down Clark Road. The clouds in the sky seemed to hover overhead, silent witnesses waiting and watching as I followed Michael toward the back door.

"Wait," I called to him. "Wait for me, Michael!" I ran across the grass and caught up with him at the steps. "Don't go in there!" I grabbed his arm, almost making him drop the bowl of salamanders.

"What's the matter with you?" Michael yanked his arm free and stared at me, almost as if he were afraid of me. "Are you going off the deep end or something?"

"There's something wrong." I stared at the back door, my heart pounding wildly and my knees shaking. "There's something in the house!"

"Molly, stop it." Michael's eyes widened behind his glasses, but he didn't move toward the door.

Before he could say more, we heard a crash from somewhere inside. Then another. As the noise increased, we clung to each other, too frightened to move.

"Let's get out of here!" Michael cried after a resounding thud from inside seemed to shake the entire house.

Running after him, I glanced back once, just in time to see a pale figure emerge from the back door. It hesitated on the steps for a moment, looking after us, then vanished.

"Did you see her?" I clutched at Michael's shirt, making him stop for a moment.

"Who?" He looked back at the house from the edge of the woods.

"Helen," I cried. "Helen! She was in the house, I saw her on the back porch."

He shook his head. "You must have seen heat waves or something," he whispered. "Whoever's in our house isn't any ghost. It's probably a motorcycle gang or something. What are we going to do, Molly?" He edged backward into the woods, putting a screen of trees and bushes be-tween us and the church. "I wish Mom would come back."

Sinking down next to him on a log, I shivered. "I know what I saw, Michael. She was standing on the porch looking at us, and laughing. Why won't you believe me?"

"Because this is the twentieth century, and I don't believe in ghosts!" His voice shook and he moved farther away from me.

"What about poltergeists? I've even read stuff in the newspaper about them. They throw fur-niture and destroy stuff, and scientists don't have any explanation for them."

"Yes, but you never see them. They cause a lot of destruction, but they don't manifest themselves the way you claim Helen does." He stood up and began walking away from me.

"Where are you going?" I leapt up and crashed through the bushes behind him.

"I think we should wait up the road for Mom and Dave. The worst thing you can do is come home while the burglars are in your house. That's how people get killed."

"She's gone now," I told him. "I saw her leave."

Ignoring me, Michael pushed through the woods, still carrying the salamanders. "It's al-most three o'clock," he said. "They should be coming along any minute."

We plunged through trailing vines of honey-suckle and stumbled out into the sunlight by the side of the road. Without saying a word to each other, we sat down in the shade and watched for the van.

After a half hour or so, I heard the sound of a motor. Jumping to my feet, I saw the van bouncing toward us: Dave at the wheel, Heather beside him, and Mom sitting in the back. He braked quickly when he saw Michael and me, kicking up a cloud of white dust.

"What is it? Is something wrong?" Mom struggled to open the side door as Michael and I jostled each other, anxious to get inside.

"Somebody broke into the house!" Michael gasped. "We heard them when we came home from the swamp."

"Are you sure?" Dave craned around from the front seat, frowning as if he thought Michael was lying.

"Of course I'm sure!" Michael leaned toward Dave, his face flushed. "They were making a lot of noise. I think they've wrecked the house."

Mom put her arm around me, holding me close, her face buried in my hair. "Thank goodness you didn't go inside," she murmured.

Dave put the van into gear and drove toward the church. "If they're still inside, I'll keep on driving into Holwell and call the police," he said.

"Don't worry, they're gone," I said, glancing at Heather as I spoke. She was looking out the window, her face turned away from Dave, smiling past her reflection at the green trees.

Sure enough, when we pulled into the driveway we saw no sign of anyone. The little church sat silent and deserted in the shade of the maples.

"It looks all right to me," Dave said. "This better not be your idea of a joke, Michael."

Michael stiffened beside me, a scowl on his face, but he didn't say anything. Silently he followed Dave up the steps and into the kitchen, with the rest of us close behind.

"It's freezing cold in here," Mom said, folding her arms across her chest and shivering.

Again I glanced at Heather, who had pushed her way to Dave's side. Catching my eye, she smiled. "I told you so, Molly," she whispered, never letting go of Dave's hand.

Dave led us down the hall. Everything seemed to be in order until we reached Michael's room. When Dave opened the door, we stepped back as cold air rushed out to meet us. Hesitating on the threshold, we stared at the room in horror. Everything that Michael cherished lay in a heap of rubble in the middle of the floor. His books, his specimen cases, his fossils and rocks, his microscope, his aquarium — all were smashed and broken, ruined. His bureau lay on its side — its drawers emptied, its mirror shattered. Not even his bed had been spared. The blankets and sheets had been hurled across the room, and the mattress leaned against a wall, his clock radio in fragments beside it.

"Oh, Michael!" Mom put her arms around him and let him cry great, gasping sobs that shook his whole body.

"My insects, my butterflies, everything's ruined," he wailed. "Everything."

Dave rested a hand awkwardly on Michael's shoulder. "The police will get to the bottom of this. Whoever is responsible will pay, believe me he will."

Then he turned to me. "We'd better take a look at your and Heather's room," he said.

But Heather was there ahead of us, sitting on her bed, still smiling. Her side of the room was untouched, but mine was destroyed. My books, my diaries and journals, my teddy bears had been ripped to bits. Like Michael's, my bed had been torn apart, my clothes scattered about, my china and glass unicorns shattered.

"They must have heard you and Michael," Dave said. "You scared them off, I guess, before they wrecked the entire house."

But I wasn't listening. Instead I was staring at a scrawled message on the wall over my bed. Written faintly in an old-fashioned hand, it said, "I have come. H.E.H."

"What did I tell you?" Heather whispered. Without my noticing, she had crept to my side. One cold hand touched my arm as she smiled up at me, her back to Dave.

Pulling away from her, I ran to Mom who was standing in the doorway, one arm around Michael. "It's all her fault," I cried. "She made this happen!"

"What are you talking about?" Mom drew me to her side.

"Good God," Dave said, exasperation darkening his voice. "Heather tries to comfort you, and you turn around and try to blame it on her." He lifted Heather, and she buried her face in his beard, sobbing.

"Molly, I can't believe you said that." Mom sounded shocked. "I know you're upset, but Heather couldn't possibly have had anything to do with this."

"Look!" I pointed at the wall. "See that?" But, even as I spoke, I saw Helen's message fade away like letters written in the sand as the tide rises. What had been words, letters were now meaningless cracks and scuffs on the wall.

"Darling," Mom drew me closer, caressing my back. "It's all right, Molly. We'll get it all put back together somehow."

Frightened, I collapsed against Mom, letting her stroke my back, my hair, crying as if I would never stop.

"We should check the rest of the house," Dave said after a while. "And our studios. Then I'll call the police."

Silently we followed him through the house. His and Mom's room, the living room, the kitchen, the bathrooms — nothing had been touched. Relieved, he walked down the driveway toward the carriage house, towing Heather behind him like a pull toy. A glance inside told him nothing had been disturbed. His bowls and mugs, his vases and platters sat on their shelves, either glazed or waiting to be glazed. The kiln and the pottery wheel stood silently in their places. Overhead in the rafters, a barn swallow twittered and flew back and forth, worried that we would disturb its nest.

Satisfied, Dave led us across the yard to the side door of the church. Once again we recoiled from the cold air, and I clasped Mom's hand, knowing what we would find.

Mom's big canvases had been slashed and thrown to the floor. Her easel was smashed, and her oil paints were smeared all over the walls. For a moment, I was sure I saw Helen's initials scrawled there, but, as before, they vanished too quickly for me to point them out.

Mom fell against Dave, too upset to speak. He put his arms around her and stroked her hair as if she were a child, letting her tears soak his shirt.

Heather hovered near her father, obviously displeased by the attention he was giving Mom.

"Don't cry, Jean, don't cry," Dave whispered. "If I can't fix the easel, I'll get you another one."

"But we can't afford it," Mom sobbed. "We were counting on the sale of my paintings to get through the winter. Now they're ruined. How will we pay the mortgage? How will we heat the house?"

"Don't worry, Jean. I can teach a few classes. And we've got insurance. I know it won't replace your paintings, but it will help." As Heather tugged at his trouser leg, he turned to her. "Not now, Heather!"

She recoiled from the anger in his voice. "You love her more than me," she whimpered.

Dave either ignored her or failed to hear. He started toward the house, his arm around Mom's shoulders. "We'll call the police," he said.

As Heather hung back, frowning at Mom and Dave, Michael turned to her. "Poor little

Heather," he said. "Left out in the cold by Daddy."

She stared up at him. "Do you believe in Helen now?" she hissed. "I told you she'd make you sorry! The next time it will be much, much worse. You just wait!"

"You little creep!" Michael grabbed her and shook her. "You know perfectly well you're lying about Helen. What makes me mad is the way you enjoy seeing us unhappy! You just love it, don't you?"

"I hate you all." Heather tried to pull away from him. "Now let me go! Let me go! Daddy! Daddy!"

Dave turned back just in time to see Heather and Michael struggling. Running toward us, he pulled Heather away from Michael. While she clung to him sobbing, he caught Michael by the neck of his tee shirt. "Don't you ever do anything like that again!" he yelled. "Aren't things bad enough without your picking on a kid half your size?"

As Dave strode back toward the house, carrying Heather, Michael and I sat down on the church steps. "I despise him," Michael muttered. "I despise them both."

"Me too." Although I didn't say it aloud, I knew I hated Helen most of all. Fearfully, I glanced toward the graveyard. For a second, I saw a glimmer of white in the shade of the oak, just a flash through the hedge. You're there, aren't you? I thought. Watching all of this, enjoying it even more than Heather.

A few minutes later, I saw the back door open. Heather ran down the steps and across the yard. Pausing at the graveyard gate, she looked at me, smiling. Then she pushed the gate open and vanished behind the hedge.

As I leaned toward Michael to tell him where Heather had gone, I was interrupted by the arrival of a police car. It pulled up by the steps, and a fat man in a light blue shirt and dark pants got out and went inside. From where Michael and I sat, we could hear his radio squawking.

Around twenty minutes later, he came outside with Mom and Dave. "It's a shame, a real shame," he was saying as he walked toward the church. "Never had anything like this happen around here before. Most folks don't even bother to lock their doors when they go out. Must have been some kids from Adelphia or somewhere. Baltimore maybe. Just passing through, doing drugs, looking for fun, who knows?"

Nodding to Michael and me, he followed Mom and Dad into the church and up the stairs to the loft. We could hear them walking around, talking. As they emerged from the church, the policeman stopped and wiped his forehead with a big handkerchief. His face was red and shiny from the heat.

"Are these the two that interrupted the vandals?" He peered down at Michael and me.

Mom introduced us, and Officer Greene asked us a few questions, but we couldn't tell him anything that would help him. As he put his notebook into his pocket, he thanked us. "You sure you didn't see anybody?" he asked.

"My sister claims she saw a ghost," Michael said, taking me completely by surprise.

"A ghost?" Officer Greene stared at me.

"Oh, Molly!" Mom touched my shoulder. "No more of that!"

Officer Greene turned to her. "Well, ma'am, she wouldn't be the first person to see a ghost at Saint Swithin's. I know grown men who don't like to drive past the graveyard at night." He chuckled. " 'Course I don't believe in ghosts myself. Never saw one and never hope to see one. But then they tell me only certain folk can see them. So who's to say?"

The officer patted my head and said that he was sorry about my room. "I hope we get it all straightened out, but I know that you'll never be able to replace some of those things."

—— ✦ 133 ✦ ——

Turning back to Mom, he added, "I'd sure hate for you folks to think anybody from Holwell made this mess. There's not a living soul in these parts who would do something like this."

As Officer Greene walked back to his car, still talking to Mom and Dave, I turned to Michael. "You were trying to make me look stupid again, weren't you?" I accused, but he didn't answer. He stood beside me, his shoulders hunched like an old man's, frowning at the ground.

"Why did you tell that policeman about Helen? He thought I was nuts!" I glared at Michael, feeling that he'd betrayed me.

Without looking at me, Michael shrugged, shoved his hands into his pockets and walked off toward the house. I watched him stop on the porch and pick up his bowl of salamanders before he vanished inside.

I sighed and sat down on the church steps. Michael was thinking about his specimens, I supposed: his butterflies, their wings carefully spread and pinned to the board, each one neatly identified; his grasshoppers and beetles and dragonflies, their fragile, dried shells and delicate wings neatly mounted under glass. It had taken him a couple of years to build his collection; he'd won a blue ribbon at the science fair last winter for the butterflies. No wonder he didn't feel like talking to me.

While I sat there, I saw Heather come out of the graveyard, a smile on her face. I turned away, not wanting to look at her. It scared me that she could summon up something as horrible as Helen and then stand there, safe beside her father, laughing at us. It made her seem as inhuman as Helen.

12

"MOLLY," MOM CALLED from the kitchen door. "Come here, honey."

Reluctantly I walked toward the house. I wasn't ready to see Heather or Dave, but I couldn't sit outside by myself forever. "What do you want?" I asked Mom.

"Let's see what we can do with your room, okay? Dave is helping Michael, and I thought I'd help you."

Unhappily I followed her down the hall, past Michael's door. Glancing in, I saw him sifting through heaps of rubbish while Dave held a black plastic garbage bag, already bulging with things broken beyond repair.

"Where's Heather?" I asked Mom as we stared about the room, wondering where to start.

"Watching television, I guess. I thought it

would be best if she stayed out of this. Having her around always increases the tension."

Silently the two of us worked, and after a couple of hours we carried the last garbage bag out. My side of the room was now stripped bare of everything I owned. It looked as impersonal as a motel room; all the things that I had collected were gone. In fact, it seemed to me that my whole personality was gone, destroyed by Helen.

"I'm going to start dinner now, Molly." Mom gave me a hug and kiss, and left me sitting on my bed trying not to cry.

A sound in the hall made me look up. Heather was standing in the doorway, staring at me. Behind her, the hall was dark and full of shadows, and I felt a tiny pinch of fear, imagining that Helen watched me over Heather's shoulder.

"What do you want?" I asked uneasily.

She took her time answering. Twisting a long, black strand of hair around her finger, she walked slowly toward me, her eyes never leaving mine. Stopping a few inches away, her face too close to mine for comfort, she whispered, "Are you going to tell who did it?"

"Who would believe me?" I shrank back against the wall, wanting to put some distance between us.

An awful little smile twitched the corners of Heather's mouth. "You believe it, though, don't you? You saw her; you saw what she wrote on your wall."

"Is she really your friend?" I stared into Heather's huge gray eyes, sure for a moment that I saw fear in them.

"We're just alike," Heather said, her voice quavering a tiny bit. "She understands me, and I understand her. She's my true sister, forever and ever."

The intensity in her face made cold chills run up and down my arms. Even the hair on the back of my neck prickled. "No, Heather," I whispered. "She's not your sister. She's evil and wicked and horrible, and you better stay away from her!" I was sitting up straight now, and my voice was rising. I grasped her thin arms, my fears for myself forgotten. "Don't go near her!"

Heather twisted away, her face pale and anxious. "Shut up, Molly, shut up!" she cried. "Helen is my friend, the only one I've ever had! Don't you dare take her away from me!"

As Heather ran out of the room, she hurled one last threat at me. "I'll tell her to come again," she cried. "And this time, she'll do something worse!"

A few minutes later, Mom called me to dinner. While we ate, I watched Heather pick at her food, eating practically nothing. Every now and then, she lifted her eyes to mine. She neither smiled nor frowned, but gazed at me till I looked away, scarcely able to eat my own chicken.

Later that evening, after the dishes were washed and put away, we all settled down in the living room. While Michael and I watched a National Geographic Special about polar bears, Mom read a novel, and Dave played checkers with Heather. After a couple of games, she climbed into his lap and fell asleep, her thumb in her mouth. With her eyes closed, she looked small and helpless, almost sweet.

As I watched Dave carry her off to bed, I promised myself that I would protect her somehow. No matter how much trouble Heather had caused, I couldn't let Helen lead her into Harper Pond. From now on, I'd try to keep an eye on her day and night.

Suddenly uneasy, I glanced at the window and the darkness it framed. A gust of wind tossed the bushes, and their branches scraped across the screen. For a moment, I thought I saw a pale face peering into the living room, silently observing us. I gasped, and the face vanished into the night as quickly as the moon slips behind a wind-blown cloud.

"What's the matter?" Michael turned to me, a piece of popcorn poised halfway to his open mouth.

"Nothing." I moved away from him, ashamed to tell him what I thought I'd seen, and snuggled next to Mom. With my head on her shoulder, I felt safe, especially when she slid her arm around me and gave me a hug.

The sound of Mr. Simmons' mower woke me in the morning. Heather's bed was empty, so I dressed quickly, anxious to keep the promise I'd made last night. She mustn't go off alone, I thought. She mustn't go to the graveyard or to Harper Pond. She mustn't go near Helen.

The kitchen was deserted, so I ate a quick breakfast and ran across the drive to the church. Mom and Dave were hard at work in the loft, trying to salvage at least some of Mom's canvases, and Heather was pouting by the window, drawing pictures in an old sketchbook. It was very hot and stuffy, and no one seemed particularly happy to see me.

"Do you want me to help?" I asked uncertainly.

"No, no," Mom said hastily. "Just take Heather outside. It's much too warm for her to stay cooped up in here."

"I'm not going anywhere with her." Heather scowled at me. "I'm staying right here with my daddy."

"But, honey," Dave said patiently. "There's nothing for you to do here. Wouldn't you rather go somewhere with Molly? You could wade in the creek or go see the cows." Dave's voice had taken on a tone of honeyed pleading. He was begging Heather to be normal, to do what ordinary little girls enjoy.

She merely stuck her lip out farther. "I like it here," she whined. "Don't you want me to be here? Don't you love me, Daddy?"

"Oh, sweetie, of course I love you." Dave left the heap of wood he had been trying to reassemble as an easel and hugged Heather. "I just thought you'd have more fun playing."

"Not with her." Heather gave me a dark look from under a cloud of black tangles. "You know how mean she is."

"Go on outside, Molly," Mom said. "Maybe you can find Michael. He said something about going down to the swamp to catch insects for a new collection."

As I left the church, I saw Mr. Simmons pushing a wheelbarrow full of grass clippings toward the compost heap. "Good morning, Molly," he called. "Is it hot enough for you?"

I nodded. It wasn't even ten o'clock and I was perspiring. "Have you seen Michael?"

He shook his head. "I brought the fishing stuff

with me, hoping he might be around, but your mother told me he left the house early to catch bugs. Quite the young naturalist, isn't he?"

Coming to a halt beside me, Mr. Simmons set the wheelbarrow down. "Do you know anything about this?" He held up a peanut butter jar full of fresh daisies. "I found them under the oak tree by that little tombstone. Third time I've seen them there."

"Heather does it," I said slowly. "She puts them there every day."

"I thought I told you kids to stay away from that end of the graveyard. Didn't I warn you about the snakes and the poison ivy?" Dumping the daisies into the wheelbarrow, Mr. Simmons paused to light his pipe. "I hear you folks had a lot of trouble here yesterday. Were robbed or something. Bob Greene says he never saw anything like it."

I stared at the flowers lying limply on top of the grass clippings. "It was horrible," I said softly. "But I don't think they'll ever catch the one who did it."

"Why not?" Mr. Simmons puffed on his pipe, waiting for me to answer.

"Well," I said, glancing toward the graveyard. "Remember the day we saw you at Harper House, and we talked about ghosts?" I searched his face, expecting him to laugh. When he didn't, I went on. "I think this graveyard is haunted too."

"I've heard folks say that. My own sister was scared to death of it, wouldn't go near it after dark. But she was always fearful, afraid of her own shadow."

I smiled; Mr. Simmons' sister sounded like me. "The policeman said people don't like to drive by here late at night." I picked up one of the daisies and twisted its green stalk around my finger.

"And what do you think, Molly?" Mr. Simmons regarded me through a cloud of sweet-smelling pipe smoke. "Have you seen anything?"

I looked down at the daisy and began to strip its petals away, one by one. She's real, she's not real, I thought as I watched the petals drift to the ground. Raising my eyes to his, I said, "I've seen Helen. And so has Heather." I paused, waiting for him to laugh, to tell me I was crazy. When he didn't say anything, I went on.

"Heather says Helen is her friend. She told Michael and me that Helen would come and make us sorry for being mean to her. It was Helen who wrecked our things yesterday. She came, just like Heather said she would." My voice was shaking now, and I had to stop. Tossing the last petal to the ground, I realized that I had ended with "She's real."

For a few seconds Mr. Simmons and I were silent. All around us, birds sang and insects chirped their summer songs, but no breeze blew. The leaves of the trees hung limply, and the sun was hot on my head and shoulders.

Finally, Mr. Simmons cleared his throat. "Why would Heather tell you something so awful?" he asked me.

"Because she hates us," I said dully, feeling ashamed, as if it were my fault somehow. "She hates Mom for taking Dave away from her, and she hates Michael and me for being Mom's children. Didn't the policeman tell you that only our stuff was destroyed? Nothing that belonged to Heather or Dave was touched."

"This is a very strange story, Molly," Mr. Simmons said. "And if I hadn't heard something like it before, I'd think you made it all up. But my own sister was convinced that our cousin Rose was led to her death in Harper Pond by the very spirit you've described to me. I didn't believe it at the time, but my sister went to her grave convinced that Rose was possessed by Helen Harper."

I stared at him, my heart thumping. "Do you think Heather is in danger?" I asked.

He fidgeted with his pipe. "Oh, it all sounds

so crazy," he said. "Especially standing here in the sunlight."

"But I've seen her," I said. "I've seen Helen."

He picked up the handles of the wheelbarrow and began pushing it toward the compost heap. "All I can say is, keep Heather away from this graveyard. Don't let her near Harper House or the pond."

For a moment I stood still, watching Mr. Simmons walk away. Then I shoved open the graveyard gate and ran toward the oak tree. Overhead, a breeze sprang up, chasing sunlight and shadows across Helen's small stone. Instinctively, I stretched my hands toward the grave and whispered, "Leave Heather alone, leave her alone."

Nothing happened. A crow flew out of the branches over my head, cawing harshly; the breeze made a dry, whispery sound in the leaves, and then all was still.

I stared at the earth mounded over Helen's grave. Beneath it was her coffin. In her coffin were her bones. I imagined her skeleton lying on its back, her skull staring up into darkness, held fast by the earth, cradled in the oak tree's roots, trapped forever.

I looked at my own arms, still outstretched, and saw the veins running blue under my skin, the bones beneath them. My skeleton. My bones. Someday they would be all that was left of me.

They would lie all alone in the dark and the cold while the years spun past, years I would never see.

I wouldn't feel the sun on my back anymore; I wouldn't hear the wind rustling the leaves; I wouldn't smell the sweet scent of honeysuckle; I wouldn't see the green grass growing over me. I wouldn't think about what I would do tomorrow. I wouldn't write any poems or read any books. All my memories would die with me, all my thoughts and ideas.

I backed away from Helen's grave. It was horrible to die, horrible. Just to think of myself ending, being gone from the earth forever, terrified me. As a shadow slanted across the tombstone, I wondered if it might not be better to live on as a ghost; at least some part of Helen remained.

Turning my back on the oak tree, I ran out of the graveyard, anxious to get away from the bones buried under my feet, but knowing I couldn't get away from the bones under my skin. No matter how fast I ran, they would always be there, always, even when I would no longer be alive to feel them.

13

TO CALM MYSELF DOWN, I took a long walk beside the creek. Although I went all the way back to the swamp, I saw no sign of Michael. Gnats and mosquitoes buzzed in clouds around my head, biting me everywhere, even through my tee shirt. I turned around and headed home, thinking Michael must have been driven away from the swamp too.

It was well after two when I walked into the kitchen to fix myself a sandwich. A note on the table told me that Mom and Dave had gone to Baltimore to shop for a new easel and replenish Mom's art supplies. They expected to be gone most of the day. "Heather is in the living room watching TV," Mom had written. "She's promised to stay in the house till you or Michael come home."

I could hear a cartoon blasting away, but when I went to ask Heather if she wanted a sandwich, I saw Bugs Bunny popping out of a magician's hat without an audience. I checked our bedroom, thinking she might be taking a nap, but she wasn't there either. Or anywhere else in the house. So much for keeping her promise, I thought as I pushed open the screen door and called her.

Instead of Heather, I saw Michael coming across the grass toward the house. He was carrying a large mayonnaise jar, and, when he saw me, he brandished it. "Look at the praying mantis I caught," he yelled. "Isn't he beautiful?"

As he thrust the jar at me, I cringed. "Get that thing away from me!"

"This is one of man's best friends." Michael gazed at me reproachfully. "He eats harmful insects. In fact, I'm going to catch some beetles for him right now. Do you want to watch him eat them?"

"Yuck." I backed away from the creature in the jar. "That's the most disgusting invitation I've ever had."

Michael shrugged. "Your loss, Molly."

"Wait a minute," I called after him. "Mom and Dave have gone to Baltimore, and I can't find Heather. Have you seen her?"

He shook his head and smiled at the praying

mantis. "Maybe this little guy thought she was a bug and ate her."

"Very funny." Angrily I watched him run off, clutching his jar, leaving me to find Heather by myself.

Although I didn't want to go back to the graveyard, I thought I might find her there. Reluctantly, I shoved the gate open and walked as far as the Berrys' marble angel. From the shelter of his outstretched wings, I saw a new jar of daisies on Helen's grave. Of Heather herself, I saw no sign.

There was, of course, only one other place to look. Harper House. Running toward the compost heap, I called Michael, thinking I could persuade him to go with me, but he had already disappeared.

As I followed the path across the field, I noticed that the horizon was ringed with clouds. They were thunderheads growing taller and darker, looming over the trees like a fleet of pirate ships. Despite the heat, I began to run. I was sure a storm was coming, and I wanted to find Heather before the thunder and lightning started.

When I reached Harper Pond, I was gasping, out of breath from running. I paused at the bottom of the hill, trying to catch my breath and ease the ache in my ribs. Above me, the ruins seemed empty, desolate. The sky showed blue behind the empty windows, and the vines billowed in a gust of wind. Uncertain of the wisdom of calling her name out loud, I scanned the walls, searching for signs of Heather: a flash of color, a sudden movement, the sound of a voice. Seeing nothing, I began climbing the hill, wishing that Michael were with me.

As I approached the house, a towering cloud drifted in front of the sun and cast everything into shadow. At the same time, a gust of wind flipped the leaves, revealing their white undersides. I knew the rain wasn't far off, and I forced myself to run toward the shelter of the bushes crowding against the ruined walls.

Burrowing through the undergrowth like a rabbit, I found myself wondering what I was doing. Heather hated me; she'd made that clear hundreds of times. And I certainly didn't love her. Or even like her. So why was I here, scrambling around in the bushes, getting scratched by thorns, scared to death of confronting a ghost? Why didn't I go home and leave Heather to Helen? After all, it was Helen she wanted, not me.

Thunder rumbled in the distance; the sky continued to darken, and the wind blew harder. Crouching in the brambles, I peered at the racing clouds, but before I could run for home, a sound from inside the house stopped me. At first

I thought it was only the wind funneling through the cracks in the walls, but the eeriness of it raised goose bumps on my arms and legs. Raising my head cautiously, I peered through the leaves screening a window just above me.

I saw Heather first. She was standing a few feet away from me, her profile turned to the window. "But I thought Daddy would be with us too," she was saying.

Scarcely daring to breathe, I peered into the shadows and saw Helen. Wearing a stained and ragged white dress, she seemed less transparent than she had in the graveyard. Her dark, lusterless hair cascaded down her back, contrasting harshly with her pale, skull-like face. Her feet were bare, and she cast no shadow. When she moved closer to Heather, she made no sound. Nothing bent or rustled when she stepped on it, and her eyes were terrible — dark and glittering and fixed upon Heather. She reminded me of a cat about to spring upon a sparrow. Merciless, without compassion or sympathy, thinking only of its own hunger.

"We don't need your father," Helen murmured. "We don't need anyone."

As she spoke, the air in the house seemed to waft toward me — cold and smelling of damp earth and stagnant water. I shivered, suddenly aware of the sound of my heart pounding loudly

with fear. I couldn't abandon Heather, not now.
I had to save her from Helen — whether she
wanted to be saved or not, whether I wanted to
save her or not.

Through my shield of leaves, I watched Helen
stretch an almost fleshless hand toward Heather,
a smile on her lips, death in her eyes. "Come,"
she said softly. "Leave this world where you are
so unhappy, where no one loves you as you want
to be loved. We'll go together, you and I."

Heather slowly put her hand in Helen's.
"You're so cold, Helen," she whispered. "Why
are you so cold?"

"Because I am alone, because nobody loves
me." Helen clung to both of Heather's hands as
ivy clings to oak, sending its roots beneath the
bark, sucking out the tree's life. "Promise you'll
never leave me; promise you'll always love me
best," she whispered fiercely.

"But what about Daddy?" Heather's eyes filled
with tears. "I can't love you more than I love
him. I can't!"

"He betrayed you, just as my mother betrayed
me. He found someone he loves more than he
loves you — *their* mother!"

The hatred in Helen's voice chilled me. I
wanted to leap up and run away from Harper
House to escape her, but I forced myself to stay
where I was, too frightened to speak or move.

"No!" Heather wailed. "No! He loves me best; I know he does!"

"Then give me my locket," Helen hissed. "I'll find someone else to give it to, someone who will love me." She held out her hand, reaching for the silver chain. "Someone who won't betray me."

Heather's fist closed over the little heart. "I want to be with you," she said, "but I want to be with Daddy, too."

"He doesn't understand you as well as I do, does he?" Helen's voice grew sweeter. "If he knew what I know, he wouldn't love you, would he?"

Heather whimpered and covered her face with her hands. Her body shook with sobs. "But I'm afraid to go in the water, Helen. I'm afraid."

"There's nothing to fear." Helen took Heather's hand. "If you don't come now, I'll go away and you'll never see me again. Never. Then what friend will you have? Michael? Molly? You know they'll never be your friends. They don't care about you. They hate you as much as you hate them."

Heather nodded her head, still sobbing, her face hidden by her hair.

"But I know all about you, Heather. Don't I? And *I* love you." Helen led Heather slowly toward the door, as if she were guiding a blind person. "It's time to go, Heather. The mermaids in the crystal palace are waiting to welcome us, to make us one of them. We'll ride on enchanted seahorses in a kingdom where the rain never falls and the rose never dies. Unicorns, elves, dragons — you'll see all the creatures I've told you about. We'll be so happy there, two princesses in our glass tower."

As I watched Helen and Heather vanish into the gloom, I yearned to enter Helen's world too. Mermaids and unicorns, crystal palaces — how I longed to see them. Eager to hear more, I pushed my way out of the bushes, heedless of the brambles scratching my legs and tangling in my hair. "Wait," I sobbed, "wait for me! Don't leave me here!"

A crash of thunder brought me to my senses. As startled as someone awakening from a beautiful dream, I cringed from the lightning that forked across the sky. As the rain began falling, I caught sight of Helen and Heather walking hand in hand toward the pond.

"Heather," I cried, but the rain fell harder, forming a silver curtain between me and the pond, hiding Heather and Helen from me.

Running down the hill, slipping and sliding on the wet grass, I reached the pond in time to see Helen leading Heather into the water. The wind blew harder, and the thunder rumbled continuously, muffling my cries.

"No, Heather, no!" I shouted as Helen led her farther from shore. Kicking off my shoes, I splashed toward them. The water was cold, and the lightning terrified me, but I plunged in deeper, trying to keep Heather in sight. It was like chasing someone into a waterfall.

When I was almost in reach of her, I tripped on a tangle of roots and splashed facedown in the pond. Sputtering and gasping, I struggled to free my feet, then looked for Heather. She was nowhere in sight. All around me, the rain poured down, and the water rose and fell in tiny waves, hiding both Heather and Helen.

Terrified, I swam toward the place I had last seen her, then dove beneath the surface, groping for an arm, a leg. Twice I came up for breath, then plunged again into the murk. Finally my fingers tangled in something I thought was an underwater weed, then recognized as Heather's hair. Grasping the long strands, I yanked her upward, struggling to get her head above water.

Holding her up, I peered through the rain, searching for the shore. I got no help from Heather. She lay still: her eyes closed, her lips blue, her hair floating around her head in dark strings.

As I got my bearings and started swimming, towing Heather, I heard a weeping sound. It wasn't the wind in the trees; it wasn't the lapping of the water — it was Helen. In front of me, behind me, to the right, to the left, sobbing and moaning, clutching at Heather with icy fingers, she begged me to give her back.

"She's mine, she's mine," Helen wept. "Don't take her from me!"

I felt a terrible chill as her fingers seized my ankles. "Give her back to me, or I'll take you both to the bottom of the pond!" she cried.

"Get away!" I kicked her viciously. "Leave us alone!"

"Give her to me!" Helen was in front of me now, so close I could see right into her horrible eyes. "You must! She has my locket and she's mine! Mine!"

"No!" My feet found the bottom, and I fumbled for the chain twisted around Heather's neck. Snapping it with my fingers, I hurled the silver heart as far as I could. As it disappeared into the rain, I cried, "There, take your locket! But not Heather — you can't have her!"

Helen moaned and turned from us to pursue the locket. Without her to slow me down, I was soon dragging Heather out of the pond. Laying her down on the ground, I crouched beside her.

She was so still, so pale. "Don't be dead, Heather," I whispered. "Please don't be dead."

Covering her mouth with mine, I tried to remember what we had learned in school about mouth-to-mouth resuscitation. Breathe, I thought, breathe! Finally she gasped and choked, opened her eyes, and stared at me. For a moment, she didn't seem to recognize me; then her eyes filled with shock. "Molly," she whispered, "Molly, what are you doing here? Where is Helen?" She twisted her head frantically from side to side, trying to locate Helen.

"She's gone," I said, glancing fearfully over my shoulder. The rain hid the pond, hid Helen — forever, I hoped.

"No," Heather cried. "No, she can't be gone. She promised to take me with her! Helen," she called out, "Helen!"

"She's gone!" I whispered, trying to hush her. "Gone!"

Heather struggled against me, trying to get up. "Let me go, Molly! I want to be with Helen, not you. Let me go!"

The rain poured down my face, blinding me, but I held on to Heather's skinny little body. Dragging her to her feet, I began climbing the hill toward the house. I had to get Heather out of the rain; I had to warm her somehow, dry her off. The church was too far away, but if I got her into Harper House we would have at least a little shelter.

"Helen, Helen," Heather shrieked. "Don't leave me." Again she tried to break away, struggling so fiercely that I could feel the bones in her arms twisting in my grip. "Let me go with my friend, my only friend," she wept piteously, suddenly collapsing against me.

"She's not your friend!" I yelled. "She tried to kill you!"

"No! No! She just wanted to take me with her. She loves me; she loves me best of all! She doesn't hate me like you do!"

"I don't hate you!" I gripped her arms tightly, my face inches from hers. "I wouldn't have pulled you out of the pond if I hated you. I'd have let you drown!"

Heather continued to sob. "If you knew me, really knew me, you'd hate me. Even Daddy would hate me if he knew everything about me." Heather looked behind her at the pond. "But she doesn't hate me. She knows everything, and she understands. We're just alike, she and I, just alike." Heather's tears mingled with the rain on her face.

"Heather," a cry came from somewhere in the rain, blown to us in the wind, a chilling and terrible cry. "Heather, where are you?"

Despite my grip, Heather broke free and ran toward the pond. "I'm coming, Helen, I'm coming!" she cried as I ran after her.

Catching up with her at the water's edge, I tackled her and threw her flat on her face in the weeds. She fought me, her wet clothes and skin making it hard to hold on to her, but she finally gave up and lay still, weeping, her body shaking with sobs.

"I can't find her," she cried. Her hand went to her throat; her fingers fumbled for the locket. "Where is it?" she cried. "What did you do with it?"

"I gave it back to her!" I peered into the rain, thinking I saw Helen's pale form hovering under a nearby willow tree. "She can't take you if you're not wearing it, can she?"

"How could you do it?" Heather wept. "How could you? My only friend, my only friend."

Struggling to my feet, I half carried, half dragged Heather toward Harper House. To my relief, she seemed to have lost her strength, her will to fight me. Faintly, I could hear Helen crying, but Heather seemed oblivious to everything. As limp as a doll, she allowed me to haul her into the ruins.

Soaked to the skin, shivering with cold, we both needed dry clothes and warmth, but the best I could do was the room Michael and I had found the last time we'd been here. At least the little bit of roof over our heads would protect us from the rain.

"This way, Heather." I guided her through the door, stepping carefully on the floorboards. "Maybe we can find matches here, light a fire or something."

My teeth were chattering so hard I could barely speak, but Heather wasn't listening anyway. Listlessly, she stared straight ahead, walking by my side like a zombie or the victim of a terrible disaster.

Halfway across the floor, I heard a splintering sound. The boards under our feet gave way and the two of us plunged downward, still holding on to each other as we fell, too frightened even to cry out.

14

TANGLED TOGETHER, Heather and I landed on a dirt floor. For a few seconds, neither of us moved nor spoke, too shocked to understand what had happened. Finally I opened my eyes and looked up. Above my head was the hole we had fallen through, its edges ragged. A gray light shone down through it, but all around us was darkness smelling of mold and damp earth and age. Shivering, I turned to Heather. "Are you all right?"

"Helen put us here," Heather whispered. "She hates me now because of you and what you did." She crouched beside me, trembling with fear and cold.

Uneasily I gazed upward at the hole, expecting to see Helen peering down at us, laughing. Nothing was there.

"Why didn't you let me go with her?" Heather

sobbed. "It sounded so beautiful. Rainbows every day, unicorns eating roses, mermaids singing — nothing ugly or hateful." Heather began sobbing again, and I put my arm around her, trying to comfort her.

She immediately stiffened and pulled away from me. "Don't touch me," she wept. "Get away from me; I don't want you near me!"

"I didn't know you were so unhappy," I said, thinking how well she'd hidden her misery behind hateful looks and nasty acts. I pulled her back against me, shocked at how small and bony she was. "Like me or not," I said, holding her tightly, "we have to stay close to each other for warmth. People can die of this kind of cold."

"I don't care if I do die," Heather sobbed. "In fact, I hope I do. Then I could be with Helen again and go to her kingdom and be happy."

"But remember, Heather, she told you your father wouldn't be there. You might hate Michael and me and even Mom, but you don't hate him. You love him."

"But what she said is true. If he knew how bad I am, he wouldn't love me anymore."

"Why do you think you're so bad, Heather?" I peered at her small white face, yearning to read the thoughts hidden behind the mask she wore. "What did you do?"

"I can't tell; I can't tell ever. Only Helen

understands." She struggled again to break away from me, but when I tightened my grip, she gave up and slumped against my side, her face hidden.

"It has something to do with the fire, doesn't it?" I stared at the dark, wet tangles of hair snaking over her shoulders. "You and Helen. Both of your mothers died in a fire."

"Don't talk about the fire!" Heather's head came up and her eyes met mine, searching, pleading.

"You started the fire." I sucked in my breath, realizing that I must have suspected it all along. "And so did she — that's it, isn't it?"

"No, no, Molly, don't say it, don't say it!" Heather put a cold hand over my mouth, trying to silence me. But it was too late. We clung to each other in the dark.

"I didn't mean to," Heather sobbed. "I was only little; I didn't know about the stove! I thought I could hide; I thought the fire would go away, but it got bigger and bigger, and Mommy was looking for me, calling me, and I didn't answer because I thought she was going to spank me. Then I didn't hear her anymore and there was smoke everywhere. A fireman came and he picked me up and carried me away, but Mommy wasn't anywhere. She wasn't anywhere, and it was all my fault, Molly!"

Heather clung to me, weeping. "Don't tell Daddy, Molly; please don't tell Daddy. Don't tell him it was me who made Mommy die. He'll hate me; he'll hate me!"

"Oh, Heather, Heather." Cradling her in my arms, I rocked her as if she were a baby. My own tears splashed down on her dark head. "It wasn't your fault, Heather. You were only three years old. Your father would never hate you, never. You didn't mean it to happen."

But she didn't say anything. She kept crying as if she would never stop. As I hugged her, I wished that I had been kinder, more understanding, instead of resenting her so much. But how could I have known she was guarding such an awful secret?

After she cried herself to sleep, I sat still and wondered what we were going to do. It was dark now. The thunder and lightning had faded away like a retreating army, leaving behind a rear guard of rain. Our clothes were beginning to dry, but we were still damp and cold. I could feel Heather shivering in her sleep.

Overhead the ruins creaked and groaned as the wind prowled through the rooms and crept through holes in the walls. Uneasily, I remembered the stones falling from the walls during Michael's and my last visit. Heather had been so sure that Helen was responsible for what happened then — and now. Had Helen really cast us down into this place, trapped us here for some awful purpose?

Heather stirred and moaned in her sleep, and I held her tighter, determined to comfort her. "It's all right, Heather," I whispered.

"I want Daddy." She opened her eyes and looked up at me. "Why hasn't he come to get us?"

"Maybe he and Mom are still in Baltimore."

"But it's dark, Molly." Heather frowned at me. "He loves Jean more than me. He doesn't care what happens to me anymore."

"You know that's not true."

"She took him away from me." Heather's voice was small and cold. She sat up and wiggled out of my embrace.

Not wanting her to slip back into that way of thinking, I shook my head. "Look, Heather, don't you think Michael and I feel the same way sometimes? We were perfectly happy living with Mom after our father left. We didn't want to share her with Dave and you, but she loves him and he loves her. They love us too. Maybe we just have to learn to be a family. All of us. You and Michael and me and Mom and Dave."

She shook her head, unconvinced. "Daddy and I were a family. Just the two of us. And Grandmother."

"Well, Michael and Mom and me were a family, too. But now we're a bigger family."

"But not better." She stuck out her lip, pouting.

"But we'll get better. Starting with you and me, Heather." I reached out and grasped her hand. "I'll be your sister, Heather, if you'll be my sister."

She regarded me soberly, examining my face for signs of deception. "And you won't tell Daddy about the fire?"

"No, I won't tell him." I paused, squeezing her hand tighter. "But I think you should."

"Oh, no, Molly." Heather jerked her hand away. "No, don't make me do that. I can't, I can't."

"But if you tell him, you'll know he loves you." I stood up, following her as she backed away from me.

"No, no," she moaned. "No."

"Come back here, Heather." I reached for her and missed as she slipped away from me, still crying. "I'm not going to make you do anything you don't want to do. All I'm saying is —" But I didn't get a chance to finish my sentence. As I lunged toward her, eager to explain, I stumbled and nearly fell.

"What's this?" I picked up a round object from a heap of rubble. When I realized what sort of eyes I was staring into, I recoiled in horror and hurled the thing into the darkness. I heard it clatter against something unseen and pulled Heather close to me, feeling her body tremble against mine.

"What was it, Molly?" she whispered.

"A skull," I gasped. "It was a human skull! I saw its eyes!"

Heather pressed her knuckles to her mouth and stared fearfully into the shadows where I had thrown the skull. "It's them," she cried. "It's them!"

"Who?" I clung to her, terrified, imagining that we were buried alive in a hideous family crypt, surrounded by the bones of Helen's victims.

"Helen's mother. And her stepfather. They were trapped in the house in the fire, and nobody ever found their bodies." Heather's voice was shaky too.

The two of us edged back to the middle of the tiny room. A little light still shone through the hole over our heads, making the shadows around us seem darker and more menacing. What other hideous things lurked there, waiting for us?

For a while neither of us spoke. The only sounds were the drip of the rain and the cheep-cheep-cheep of a cricket. The small, cheerful noise seemed very out of place in our grim surroundings.

"Heather," I said, breaking the silence at last. "Did Helen start the fire?"

She nodded. "But she didn't mean to. She was arguing with her stepfather and she knocked an oil lamp over. The tablecloth and the drapes caught fire, and Helen ran out of the room. The fire spread so fast; it trapped her mother and her stepfather. Helen heard her mother calling her, and then the floor caved in. She ran outside, into the pond." Heather hid her face in her hands and wept. "She's been alone ever since, Molly."

"But the other little girls, the ones who drowned in the pond." I leaned toward Heather. "What happened to them? Why aren't they with her?"

"They wouldn't stay. They always faded away and left her. She doesn't know where they went. To their parents maybe. They didn't love her enough to stay." Heather leaned against me, sobbing. "And now I've left her too, and she's still alone."

I stroked her hair and tried to comfort her, wishing Mom were here. Surely she and Dave had returned from Baltimore and noticed that we were missing. Why hadn't they come to rescue us?

"I'm so cold," Heather whimpered. "So cold."

The temperature seemed to be plummeting,

and the air smelled more strongly of decay and stagnation. A glimmer of light drew my attention to the hole above us. Helen was kneeling on the floor, peering down at us. The silver chain hung from her neck, the heart slowly turning, reflecting the bluish glow of her skin.

"It was my fault," Helen cried, stretching out her hands. "My fault, Mama."

Heather looked up, then shrank against me, her bony shoulder blades jabbing against my chest. "I don't want to go with her anymore, Molly," she whispered. "Don't let her take me."

I held her tightly. "Don't worry," I whispered. "I'll protect you."

"Mama, Mama, I'm sorry," Helen wailed above us. She looked more tragic than frightening, and I ached with pity for her. She seemed unaware of Heather and me. All that existed for her was her own sorrow. Slowly she dropped down through the hole and glided past us into the shadows where I'd hurled the skull. Dropping to her knees, she whispered, "Forgive me, Mama, forgive me."

She paused. In the glow she cast, I could see two skeletons. Extending her hand, she reached out toward them. "And you too, Papa Robert. I didn't mean for you to die. Nor Mama either. Nor me, nor me."

She knelt motionless by the skeletons, her head bowed, weeping. Heather's hand closed around mine. "Poor Helen," she whispered.

As I watched, another figure appeared in the cellar. From mist it seemed to form itself into a woman wearing a long dress. Smiling, she drew Helen to her feet and embraced her, comforting her, stroking her hair, rocking her gently. For several seconds, the two figures shimmered in the darkness. Then they disappeared as quickly as images on a screen vanish when the projector is turned off. Slowly the terrible cold subsided, and I knew that Heather and I were alone and out of danger.

"It was Helen's mother," I whispered.

Heather squeezed my hand. "She forgave her, Molly; she forgave her." She looked up at me and smiled. "She knew it was an accident; she knew Helen didn't mean for them to die."

"I know." I returned the squeeze, marveling at the tiny bones in her hand.

"Helen isn't alone anymore. She isn't sad." Heather gazed at me. "Do you think my mother has forgiven me?"

"Oh, Heather, she forgave you long ago."

"And Daddy — if I tell him, do you think he'll forgive me?"

"I'm sure he will."

Heather relaxed and leaned against me, her

thumb seeking her mouth. "I wish he would come and get us," she sighed. "I want to go home."

"So do I." I toyed with her hair, twining it round my finger. It was dry now, silky soft against my skin. Tonight, I thought, when we were safely home, I would brush it for her till it shone.

15

—❖—

HOURS SEEMED TO PASS while Heather slept. The rain stopped. Above my head, I could see a few stars through the holes in the roof. From somewhere in the woods an owl hooted, and the cricket continued to chirp, safe in his hiding place. Just as I was falling asleep, I heard Michael calling me.

Nudging Heather awake, I jumped to my feet. "Down here!" I yelled. "We're down here!"

I heard someone enter the room above us. "Careful," I shouted, "the floor's weak. Heather and I fell through."

A flashlight beamed down on Heather and me, and Michael yelled, "Dave, here they are!"

In a moment, Dave was lowering himself cautiously through the hole. Embracing Heather, he cried, "You're all right, thank God you're all right."

"Molly saved me," Heather said, clinging to him. "I almost drowned in the pond, and she saved me."

Dave put an arm around me and hugged me against his side, with Heather between us. "We've been so worried. What were you doing here?"

Before I could answer, I heard Michael gasp, "There's bones down there!" He was crouching above us, beaming his flashlight into the corner where the skeletons lay. In the circle of light, we saw them huddled together, still wearing the rags of their clothing.

"They've been here ever since the fire," I told Dave.

"They're Helen's parents," Heather added. "You don't have to worry, Daddy; they won't hurt you."

Dave did look a little edgy, I thought. "Let's get you home," he said to Heather. "You too, Molly." He hoisted Heather onto the floor above us, and Michael helped her to her feet. Then Dave boosted me up, and pulled himself up after me.

"Oh, Molly." Mom was kneeling in the doorway, her arms around Heather. She reached out for me and I ran to her, clinging to her as shamelessly as a baby. "I've been so scared," Mom said, hugging me tightly.

Dave picked up Heather and turned back to

Michael. "Come on," he said. "The girls need to get home and have a nice hot bath."

Michael was still peering into the darkness of the cellar, playing the beam of his flashlight on the bones. "Isn't it against the law to leave bones lying around unburied?" he asked Mom.

She moved cautiously to his side and looked over his shoulder. "They were buried," she said uncertainly, "till now."

"I'd guess that nobody knew the cellar was there," Michael mused. "Most of the ceiling fell down and blocked this room. If you all hadn't fallen through the floor, those bones would have lain there forever."

Dave nodded. He was still standing in the doorway, holding Heather. "I'll call the police when we get back to the church," he said. "They ought to be given a decent burial."

"Couldn't I keep them?" Michael asked. "I could study them, learn all about them. It would be a great science project!"

"Michael!" Mom stared at her offspring, obviously shocked.

"Well, they have bones in science class. And medical students study them. Why can't I? It's scientific."

"They have to be buried with Helen," Heather said. "Families are always buried together."

"Like the Berrys," I said, walking out of the house with Mom.

"What are you two talking about?" Dave asked.

"You know that little tombstone in the grave-yard?" I watched Michael, waiting for him to make a derogatory remark about ghosts. But he was absorbed in shining his flashlight far ahead, watching its beam fan out into a circle as he played it across the woods.

"Well," I went on, "Helen Harper is buried there. She lived in this house, and when it burned down, her parents died. Their bones are in the cellar, but they should be buried with Helen, like Heather says."

Heather and I looked at each other, firmly united. "Please, Daddy, tell the police so they'll know," she said.

"It's very important to you, isn't it?" Dave hugged Heather and she nodded.

"It's important to Helen, too," she said. "And Molly."

Dave smiled at me. "Is this some sort of an alliance?"

Slipping my arm around Mom's waist, I smiled back. "It sure is," I said.

When we got home, Heather and I each had a hot bath and steaming cups of herb tea before we went to bed. After Dave and Mom said good-night and left us alone in the dark, Heather said, "I'm sorry I told Helen to wreck your things, Molly. If I could, I'd make her come back and fix everything. Your stuff, and Michael's and Jean's, too."

"It's all right, Heather. It wasn't your fault. Helen possessed you, I think."

"But not anymore," Heather said.

"No, she's gone now."

"With her mother." Heather yawned.

"And her stepfather," I added. "They're a family now." A little whisper of a breeze puffed the curtains away from the window and set the leaves to murmuring.

"Should I tell Daddy about the fire tomorrow?" Heather asked quietly.

"I think you'll feel better if you do."

"Will he still love me?" Her voice quivered.

"I know he will. You saw Helen's mother, the way she hugged her and comforted her. She forgave her. And she hadn't stopped loving her."

Heather sighed and turned over noisily. "I'm glad you're my sister, Molly," she said, her voice slurry with sleep.

"Me, too, Heather." I meant it. For the first time, she seemed like a real, true sister instead of an enemy camping in our home, making me and everyone else miserable.

The next morning, Dave called the police and told them about the skeletons in Harper House. Although he had to do a lot of explaining, he finally succeeded in convincing Officer Greene that the bones should be buried in Saint Swithin's Churchyard, as close to Helen's as possible. When he hung up the phone, Heather ran to his side and slipped her hand in his.

"Will you go for a walk with me, Daddy?" she asked. "I need to talk to you about something."

I could hear the fear in her voice, but Dave didn't seem to notice. "Sure, honey," he said. "I've got work to do in the carriage house, but I can spare you a few minutes before I get started."

I stood at the back door and watched them walk across the yard together, her face turned up to his, his bent down toward hers. Mom stood behind me, looking over my shoulder.

"I don't know why," she said, "but Heather seems happier this morning. And last night she really surprised me. She actually let me hug her. Maybe your adventure together at Harper House was just what this family needed to pull it together."

I leaned against her, enjoying the feel of her

arms around me. "Would you still love me no matter what I did?"

"What do you mean?" Mom asked.

"Well . . ." I watched a monarch butterfly fly toward the zinnias growing in a tub near the porch. "Suppose I did something really horrible and I told you about it a long time afterward? Would you hate me?" I pulled away from her so I could see her face.

Mom smiled, but she seemed a little puzzled. "Are you about to confess to committing a heinous crime?" She made it sound as if she were joking. "*You* were the one who broke your grandmother's priceless Ming vase all those years ago!" she laughed.

"No, Mom. I'm serious." I studied her eyes, trying to read the expression in them. "Suppose I caused somebody to die. I didn't mean to; it was an accident. But I was scared to tell you. What would you do if I confessed?"

Mom brushed a strand of hair out of my eyes, her hand touching me gently. "Molly, you're not making any sense," she said slowly.

"Would you still love me? Would you forgive me?" I heard my voice rise like a child's. "That's all I want to know. Do parents love their children no matter what they do?"

Mom put her arm around me and hugged me.

"I'll always love you, Molly, always — no matter what. You should know that by now."

"But how about Dave? Would he?"

"Dave?" Mom hesitated as if she weren't sure how Dave fit into all this.

"Not me. Heather. If Heather did something awful, would he still love her?"

"Molly," Mom said, sucking her breath in hard, her eyes darkening with concern. "What are you trying to tell me?"

"The fire — Heather started it by accident, but she thinks it's her fault her mother died." The words flew out of me as if a dam had burst. "She's afraid Dave will hate her if she tells him."

"Oh, my God." Mom leaned against the door frame, her hands pressed to her mouth. "That poor little girl, that poor, poor child. To keep something like that bottled up inside all these years. No wonder she's been so closed off and untouchable."

"She was playing with the stove," I told Mom. "Somehow a fire started. She hid, and her mother died looking for her, I guess. She told me about it last night when we were trapped in the cellar. I thought she should tell Dave."

"Is that why she wanted to go for a walk?" Mom stepped out on the porch and gazed across the lawn. "I don't see them anywhere," she said.

"I gave her the right advice, didn't I?" I looked past Mom's still figure toward the graveyard, imagining Heather and Dave sitting near Helen's grave as she told him about the fire.

Mom turned back to me, embracing me fiercely. "Of course you did, Molly. Dave will understand."

Releasing me, she shook her head. "I never even suspected," she said, more to herself than to me. "She must have thought we'd all hate her if we knew."

"That's exactly what she did think."

"And the ghost — it must have been a projection of her own guilt," Mom said.

Before I could think of a good answer, I saw Heather and Dave walking toward us. He was still holding her hand, and they were smiling at each other. When she saw us, Heather pulled away and ran to me, her eyes shining with tears. As Mom hurried to Dave's side, Heather smiled at me.

"I told him everything, Molly," she whispered, "and he still loves me. He knows it was an accident." Burying her head in my stomach, she knotted her skinny arms around me and squeezed till it hurt.

A few days later, Plummer's Funeral Parlor sent a hearse to Saint Swithin's Graveyard. For the first time in almost forty years, the crows in the oak tree had a funeral to watch.

Mr. Simmons himself had supervised the digging of the graves. The minister from the new church was there, Bible in hand, and a number of people from Holwell, including a reporter for the *Journal*. It was almost a festive occasion, I thought, as I listened to the conversations around me. Most of these people knew nothing of the terrible unhappiness that the burial was bringing to an end.

At the conclusion of the service, everyone stepped forward, picked up a handful of earth and tossed it into the graves. I heard several of them comment on Heather's tears.

"What a sensitive child she must be," a stout lady observed, adjusting the angle of her large straw hat.

Her companion nodded. "You'd think she knew the poor souls personally."

"She's probably too young to be exposed to something as tragic as a funeral," the woman in the straw hat said. "I've never thought little children should be told about death. Why frighten them? Let them keep their innocence as long as they can."

The two of them walked to their car and drove off, leaving us alone, except for Mr. Simmons. "Glad to see this settled," he said, heaping the earth over the graves. "She'll rest in peace now, like them." He waved the shovel toward the Berry Patch. "She's with her own."

Heather gazed at the marble angel poised on his pedestal above the Berrys, his wings uplifted. "Daddy should make Helen one of those," she said to me. "I think she'd like to have one, don't you?"

"It would look very pretty," I said, watching Mr. Simmons pat the freshly-turned earth with his shovel.

By September, a small marble angel guarded Helen's grave, and two stones flanked hers. Her own name, not just her initials, marked her burial place, and English ivy softened the mounds of earth over her parents' graves. The cemetery had lost its gloom, and I no longer feared it.

One afternoon in early October, Michael, Heather, and I were sitting in a sunny spot not far from Helen's grave. It was a warm, sweet-smelling day, more like spring than fall. Michael was watching a huge wood beetle crawling around in its glass-jar prison, and I was reading *The Borrowers* to Heather.

"Do you want me to read the next chapter?" I was sure she wouldn't want me to leave poor Stainless facing certain capture, but when I looked at her I realized she hadn't been paying much attention to the story.

She was lying on her back, chewing on a blade of grass and staring up at the clouds drifting slowly across the incredibly blue sky. "Do you think she can see us from where she is?" she asked dreamily, her mind apparently far from Stainless' plight.

"I don't know," I said, guessing that she was thinking of Helen. It was the first time in weeks that she had mentioned her. "Wherever she is, though, she's happy," I added. "I'm sure of it."

"Me too," Heather agreed. She sat up and gazed at the angel under the oak tree. He gazed back serenely, seeming to return her smile. Suddenly she grasped my arm, her nails biting through the sleeve of my shirt. "Molly," she whispered. "Look."

She got to her feet and ran toward the angel, and I ran after her, seeing what she saw. Something shiny dangled from the angel's outstretched hand: a silver locket turning slightly in the breeze.

Before I could stop her, Heather snatched the chain from the angel's stiff fingers. As I watched, it seemed to pop open by itself in her outstretched palm. On one side was a picture of Helen. On the other was a folded piece of paper.

With trembling fingers, Heather slipped it out of the frame and spread it flat. We both read the message, written in the same hand I had once seen scrawled on my bedroom wall: "With love from Helen," it said. "Do not forget me."

Heather and I looked at each other. The sun warmed our backs as it shone down through the oak's reddening leaves. Bees buzzed in the goldenrod and a grasshopper bounded away from Michael as he approached us.

"Where did you get that old thing?" he asked, looking at the locket. "I thought you lost it last summer."

"Helen gave it back to me," Heather told him solemnly. "It's all right for me to wear it now," she added, looking at me. "Isn't it?"

I nodded, but Michael rolled his eyes skyward. "Not Helen again. I thought we'd heard the last of that ghost stuff."

"I think we have," I said. "Now."

Silently Heather fastened the chain around her neck, smiling at me as she did so. Together we walked out of the graveyard. Behind us, Michael kicked at the grass.

"I still don't believe it," I heard him yell at our backs, but it seemed to me that his voice quavered a tiny bit.